HOMICIDAL HOLIDAY

SAM CHEEVER

ELECTRIC PROSE PUBLICATIONS

It was a simple holiday getaway...a chance to regroup and figure out how to move forward after losing the man of her dreams...then she witnessed a murder on the beach...

Dolfe Honeybun broke up with Blaise Runa because her party girl ways were driving him to distraction. Unfortunately, out of sight does NOT mean out of mind. And when his favorite party girl sees something she shouldn't and finds herself being chased by a cold-blooded killer, reason shuts down and Dolfe's heart takes over. If only he can get to her in time!

1

olfe Honeybun stood in the shadows and watched his ex-girlfriend flirt with a tall, annoyingly good looking guy on line at a popular nightclub. She looked spectacular as usual; her long, slimly curved form lovingly embraced in some kind of shimmery white material which didn't cover nearly enough of her.

He frowned as the man she was speaking to leaned forward, whispering something into Blaise's ear as his hand slipped over her hip and stopped on her firm, round behind. Dolfe's pressure spiked and he was moving forward before he could stop himself.

He crossed the street to the blare of horns, almost entirely oblivious to oncoming traffic. Red flares were flashing in front of his eyes and his hands were clenched into fists. As he plummeted heart first into complete loss of control, Dolfe took some comfort in the fact he hadn't pulled his gun.

It didn't matter that Blaise deftly, and with a smile, removed the man's hand from her butt. It didn't even matter that she walked away. Because the other guy's lust-saturated gaze followed her sexy sway down the sidewalk, her heels click-clacking rhythmically on the concrete as she walked.

Dolfe decided at that moment the man had to die.

He headed straight for the cocky, overdressed buffoon who was accepting knuckle bumps from his friends by way of celebrating that he'd copped a feel from the gorgeous black woman with the million dollar smile.

Dolfe would rip him into such small pieces his friend Brita Muldane, the cop, wouldn't even be able to find the body.

The weasel turned as Dolfe stormed toward him, his unintelligent blue eyes widening at the look on Dolfe's face. He took a step back as Dolfe reached for him.

Dolfe's ears roared. He could taste every beat of his heart as his pulse surged to the danger zone. And adrenaline had him by the throat as he grabbed pretty boy's expensive tweed coat by the lapels and dragged him off the ground.

"Hey!" the guy's friends coughed out. But when Dolfe turned his murderous gaze on them, they lifted their hands and stepped back. Apparently judging their friend to be unworthy of having their own blood spilled.

Somewhere on the edges of Dolfe's awareness a familiar click, clack, click, clack intruded, the sound speeding and getting louder as it got closer.

He shook the offensive pup like a rag doll and pressed his face close. The young punk stank of expensive cologne. He was darn lucky he didn't smell like Blaise.

That would have signed his death warrant for sure.

Click, clack, click, clack...

The guy tried tugging Dolfe's hands from his coat without any success. "What the hell, man?"

"You think that's the right way to treat a lady?" Dolfe growled into his face.

The guy blinked under every word, as if he were being pelted with buckshot. "What lady?"

Dolfe's growl deepened and the guy's heels lifted another inch from the ground. "Wrong response, punk."

Click, clack, click, clack...

"Hey come on, dude," the guy whined. "Blaise is just a friend."

"You always run your hands all over your friends' asses?" Chuckling from the guy's disloyal friends abruptly stopped as Dolfe skimmed them with a hostile, green glance. When they were properly quelled, Dolfe refocused his hostility where it belonged. "You want to feel up *my* behind?"

More chuckling.

Click, clack, click, clack...

The guy grimaced. "I don't play for that team, dude."

Dolfe shook him. "But I thought you always felt up your friends. I'm thinking you and me are friends."

"Darn it, Dolfe!" A soft, long-fingered hand gripped his arm, tugging on it. "Let him go."

Dolfe inhaled deeply, her exquisite scent spearing his senses and rolling like warm butter over his nerves. "Stay out of this, honey. The guy dissed you. I'm takin' care of it."

She tugged harder. "Dolfe Honeybun, you let go of him right now and come with me."

He finally turned to look at her and forgot to breathe. He'd almost forgotten how beautiful she was...how delicious she looked and smelled. He frowned, turning back to the punk. "Learn respect you little jerk." He dragged the guy off the ground another half inch just to drive home his point and then flung him away.

The punky kid stumbled backward several steps, his friends catching him before he landed on his ass.

Dolfe turned away and immediately forgot him. He grinned. "Hey, honey. You look stunning as always."

Blaise glared at him, her long, slender arms crossed over her chest. Her pretty brown eyes flashed with anger. "Let's take a little walk, shall we?" She started down the sidewalk, her four inch high spiked heels click-clacking angrily against the concrete.

Dolfe winked at the disgruntled punk and started after her, his gaze sliding over the crowd of males to ensure nobody else got any ideas about disrespecting his girl.

He blinked, his stomach twisting with disappointment. Scratch that. Blaise was now his ex-girlfriend. They'd broken up the week before. Primarily because of the very thing he'd just interrupted.

Blaise hit the corner and stopped, turning back to him with a decidedly unhappy look on her beautiful face. The golden light from the streetlamp illuminated her delightful form, making her look like an ebony-skinned angel with fire in her veins. She fairly vibrated with rage. Her whole frame was taut with it, her delicate jaw working over the words she no doubt wanted to fling his way.

She didn't even wait for him to reach her before she launched. "What is wrong with you? What are you doing stalking me?"

Dolfe drifted to a stop and shoved his hands into his pockets, holding her fiery gaze. He was fully aware he'd acted badly, but he didn't care. He'd do it again in a heartbeat.

She didn't seem to require a response from him anyway. She was too busy pelting him with her angry verbal assault. "We broke up, remember? We're no longer an item, you and I. We're finished, *kaput, finito*." She stepped closer, poking him in the chest with every word. "I don't answer to you anymore and if I want to flirt with another guy I'll do it all day long. *Capiche*?"

He lifted an eyebrow and crossed his arms, telling himself the tearing sensation in his chest cavity was just the aftermath of a bad lunch burrito. Unfortunately, he knew better.

She was flailing his heart into tiny little pieces. "I'm sorry, honey. But I'm not gonna just stand around and watch some punk manhandle you on the street."

She took a deep breath and expelled it, obviously striving for calm. "I had it handled, Dolfe."

He shook his head. "No, no you didn't. You sweetly removed his hand and smiled at him. Kneeing him in the crotch would be handling it. What you did was just short of a promise."

"Shut up, Honeybun."

He twisted his lips against a cocky response and glanced away, knowing she deserved better. She had a right to be mad. "I don't regret what I did."

"I'm sure you don't. That's the problem."

He covered the last of the distance between them and wrapped an arm around her tiny waist, pulling her close. She gasped in surprise and struggled against his grip. "No. The *problem* is that I can't stand the idea of you with another guy. The *problem* is that you should be in my bed right now, writhing and moaning underneath me." Her eyes glittered with unshed tears and he suddenly felt guilty for dragging them both through the mire again. Dolfe lowered his head so that her lush lips were close... too close. Close enough for him to feel the soft hitch in her breath that told him she wasn't nearly as disinterested as she pretended. "The *problem* is that you make me crazy and the longer we're together the crazier I get." Dolfe touched her lips in a soft, prolonged kiss and then forced himself to step back. "I wasn't stalking you." He scrubbed a hand over his chin because he needed to do something with it. If he didn't, he'd be grabbing her up again and he wasn't sure he'd be able to let her go a second time. "I'm working."

She frowned. "I'm supposed to believe you just happened to show up at the same club where I was?"

Dolfe turned away. "Believe it or not. I've been here for two hours, watching for the most likely cheating spouse of my client." He looked around. "I'll walk you to your car. Where did you park?"

She stepped past him. "I'm going back to the club."

Anger spiked and Dolfe gritted his teeth against it. She was right. They weren't together anymore. It sucked planet-sized lemons but it was the reality he'd have to get used to. After all, it had been his idea to split. He didn't respond as she walked away... didn't trust himself to speak. Instead, he followed along behind to make sure she got safely inside, the click, clack, click, clack of her heels pinging against his nerves like bullets. And doing just as much damage to his heart.

"Are you sure you're up for this?"

Blaise turned to the man sitting next to her, forcing a smile onto her face. "Of course. Why?"

Dugald Richards shrugged, his dark chocolate gaze sliding over her assessingly. "You don't seem very excited about our trip."

Blaise reached over and squeezed his arm. The bulging flesh was like iron under her fingers. It reminded her of Dolfe. She barely kept from sighing, biting her bottom lip instead. Everything reminded her of Dolfe. "I'm just a little tired." She *was* tired, in fact she'd been tired for two weeks, since Dolfe had told her he couldn't be with her anymore. She was starting to think it was depression. Which was why when her best friend since high school asked her if she wanted to come to Florida with him over Christmas she eagerly agreed.

Maybe some sun and partying would make her feel better. The plane's engines roared as they prepared to land in Miami and the pilot came on the intercom to verify that they would be on the ground in ten minutes.

Still, the prospect of parties just didn't give her the jolt of excitement it used to. It was the constant partying that had come between her and Dolfe. He was a serious man. A man whose job as a private investigator meant he was always dealing with the seedier side of life. Dolfe knew intimately how dangerous the world could be. He lived it every day. He'd seemed fascinated by her carefree, party girl ways in the beginning. But after a few months, her almost manic need for fun and frivolity started to rub him the wrong way.

Blaise knew he had a point. She was careless at times. Unthinking. But she was young and beautiful and she wanted to enjoy it while she could.

Unfortunately, she wasn't enjoying it anymore.

Scrunched into the comparatively tiny Business Class seat, Dugald wrapped his long fingers around her hand and squeezed. "Reggie and the gang are meeting us at the hotel in an hour. We'll have dinner and drinks on the terrace and then go to a party they say is *the* big event of the season." He tried to stretch his long, long legs and grimaced as his knees bumped up against the seat in front of him.

Blaise dug for some enthusiasm and tried to

focus it into her answering smile. "That sounds perfect. I want to walk on the beach every day while we're here. And eat seafood until it's coming out my ears."

Dugald laughed his baritone laugh. "None of that fishy stuff for me. I'm gonna eat Cuban food until my eyes turn the color of peppers."

The steward started down the aisle, collecting trash and telling people to close their trays in preparation for landing. Dugald adjusted his seat into the upright position as the steward lifted a sandy blond eyebrow at him. Her friend saluted and made the guy laugh. Blaise grinned. He was always making people smile. It was his best skill other than playing basketball, which he'd done professionally for six years until the Indiana Pacers had cut him from the roster the previous year.

Dugald had taken the change with his usual grace and good humor. He'd always wanted to open a restaurant, he told Blaise. So that was what he'd done.

Not surprisingly for anybody who knew him, *Dugald's* was on its way to becoming an Indianapolis favorite. Partly because it was a favorite spot for the Pacers players and management to hang out. And partly because of Dugald himself. Like Blaise, her friend loved people and he was good with them.

She'd been a little surprised when he'd asked her to come with him to Florida. The holiday season was a busy time in the restaurant. But Dugald had a good manager he trusted, and he said he needed a break.

Lord knew Blaise needed one too. She only hoped the time away would help her forget the way Dolfe's hands had felt on her body...or the decadent delights his sexy mouth performed on her.

Blaise's body tightened on the thought and her mood took a dip. She pushed the painful thoughts away. Dolfe no longer wanted to be with her. He'd moved on. And she was determined to move on too. She'd even formed a plan for how to do that, and her current trip might be just the thing she needed to put that plan into play, turning Dolfe Honeybun and their short but incendiary relationship into a distant memory. As Blaise left the 737 and stepped into the busy Miami terminal, taking Dugald's muscled ebony arm, the thought made her feel a little bit better.

2

"Come on, cuz, I really think you'll love Angelique. Emma says she's just your type."

Dolfe shook his head. "I refuse to be the sad, pathetic object of your woman's matchmaking attempts, Clovis."

His cousin grinned, his gray-blue eyes sparking with good humor. "I've seen her, soldier. She's gorgeous. And she's smart too. She just passed the bar and wants to be a prosecutor." Clovis worked the single crutch with wicked skill as he descended his new deck into the freshly mown backyard of his big old farmhouse. Blown off his feet by an IED in a rescue operation for Dolfe's dad, Senator Brick Honeybun, Clovis had spent the last six months getting his legs back under him...literally...after a bruised spine injury had put him in a wheelchair. But nothing kept the ex-Marine down for long.

Though he was still required to use the crutch for a few more months while the injury continued to heal, Clovis's brother, Godric, a talented surgeon, had declared Clovis well on the road to a complete recovery.

Clovis had been a terrible patient and a wonderful one at the same time. His impatience and determination to return to normal had driven his physical therapist crazy but had probably been the biggest reason he'd recovered so quickly.

Dolfe eyed the petite black woman working her way toward them with an empty tray. Though Dolfe doubted she even noticed *him*. Emma Banks had eyes only for Clovis. And a smile that would melt the most hardened man's heart.

Dolfe could almost hear Clovis's heart melting as the pretty young mother stopped in front of him and lifted to her toes to kiss his lips. "Hello, soldier."

Clovis grinned, saluting her crisply. "Are my recruits on the grill as commanded?"

Emma rolled her eyes. "The *hamburgers* are on the grill. Cilla helped me."

Clovis's grin widened. "Are they in pieces?"

She bit her bottom lip to keep from laughing, but her pretty brown eyes sparkled with it. "A few of them might be considered bite-sized now. I was thinking I'd bring out some slider buns."

Clovis laughed and Dolfe chuckled with him.

"Clovish!" A pretty little girl bounced up to them

and flung her tiny arms around Clovis's legs. "I hepped mama cook."

Dolfe watched in awe as his big, gruff cousin visibly melted. Clovis cupped the girl's tiny head in a big paw. "Good work, soldier. Do you want to help me carry them inside when they're done?"

Little Pricilla jumped up and down. "Yeth!"

Then one tiny hand flew up to her creamy brown forehead and Dolfe's eyes widened as the five-year-old saluted.

Clovis winked at Emma and took the little girl's hand. "Let's go make sure your mama didn't mess them up."

Emma smacked him on the behind as he and the little girl headed toward the grill.

"He looks great," Dolfe said. "You've done wonders with him."

Emma laughed, shaking her head. "I've done nothing but love him. He's done all the work."

Dolfe knew better. Clovis had told him how the tiny spitfire he'd fallen in love with had harangued and encouraged and shamed him to keep his head in the game.

Clovis was used to being strong...invincible...and his injury had really set him back on his heels, emotionally as well as physically. It had been up to Emma to show him that strength comes in forms other than densely-muscled limbs. Something Dolfe suspected she'd learned early and often as a single mother.

Emma dragged her gaze away from Clovis and fixed Dolfe with an intense stare. Terror slid up his spine. "Now, about Angelique..."

Dolfe lifted his hands, taking a step back. "No matchmaking."

She frowned. "You'll love her, I promise."

He shook his head, looking at the ground.

A soft hand touched his arm. "I know your heart is broken."

He closed his eyes. "I broke up with *her*, Emma."

"That doesn't make it hurt any less."

He sighed, nodding. "I won't lie. I'm still pretty torn up about it." He lifted his gaze to her. "I worry about her, you know. She has zero sense of self-preservation."

Emma patted his arm. "You'd be surprised. She's not stupid, Dolfe. And she's a grown woman. You need to let her make her own mistakes and trust that she can find her way around them."

He frowned. "Yeah. I know you're right."

"But you're not gonna listen, are you?"

He dropped an arm around her slim shoulders. "Don't you have enough to do keeping that one on the straight and narrow?"

She blew a raspberry. "There's no keeping him anywhere he doesn't want to be, Dolfe. You should know that by now."

"I do know that. Which is why the fact that he's putty in your hands is just so fascinating."

She looked embarrassed. "I don't know about that. But I love him to death." Her brown gaze sparkled with unshed tears. "And Cilla worships him. I'm really lucky."

When Dolfe didn't respond, she turned to him. "Oh god. I'm so sorry. It's really rude of me to talk about how happy I am..."

Dolfe shook his head, giving her shoulders a squeeze before stepping away. "Don't be ridiculous. You and Clovis deserve this. You've more than earned it."

She didn't look convinced, but fortunately the screen door to the house slammed and voices called out to them.

The rest of the Honeybun clan was arriving. Saving Dolfe from a conversation that had all but flayed his gut into strings.

The night was thick and moist despite the fact that the sun had dropped below the horizon hours earlier. The sand beneath Blaise's feet was still warm, the granules heavy and dry as they rolled under her step.

Behind her a dense fringe of palm trees turned the multi-hued lighting of the party to colored ribbons on the sky, which swayed and twisted at the whim of the gently blowing trees. The palms muted the loud music and transformed the raucous conversation to a formless rumble.

Blaise headed for the water, swinging her shoes as she walked. They were her favorite party shoes, tall and elegant and cherry red. Jimmy Choos. Against her will, her thoughts turned to another pair of Jimmies she'd worn the night she'd come upon a tall, broad-shouldered god with a square jaw and intense green gaze.

Dolfe had tripped over her in the dark that night, skidding several feet on a filthy warehouse floor. But he'd come up with a flashlight and a big, black gun in his hands and Blaise had nearly peed herself when he spoke.

Don't you freaking move!

Thinking of their meeting now, Blaise found herself smiling. Those first moments characterized the entirety of their relationship. With him trying to understand why she was drunk and barefoot in a meth lab, carrying her unpractical shoes in one hand while her foot bled from being cut on the broken glass scattered all over the floor, and Blaise thoroughly enjoying his confusion while contemplating how his sexy lips would taste and feel.

Dolfe Honeybun was as serious as bullet. And Blaise was a party girl, viewing life through a brightly colored lens that highlighted its many possibilities.

They were polar opposites, her and Dolfe. Yet she felt his loss like a hole in the pit of her stomach. She figured it would take a really long time to get over him.

No matter how many parties she attended.

A shout down the beach brought her head up and her attention back to the moment. She glanced in that direction but the night was too dark, the stingy moon hiding behind a charcoal gray bank of quickly skidding clouds.

She turned away, heading the opposite direction to avoid meeting up with whoever had given the drunken shout.

Blaise wasn't in the mood for company. It was the reason she'd skipped out on the party in the first place. She just wanted to walk on the beach for a while, letting the rhythmic roar of the water lull her thoughts and ease the sudden, inexplicable panic that had slashed through her back at the bar, where her friends, new and old, still partied.

They probably hadn't even noticed she didn't come back from the ladies. The thought brought sadness sliding through her and, to her amazement, Blaise's eyes filled with tears. She suddenly felt alone and lonely.

The realization stopped her, dropping her to her knees in the warm sand.

She'd never felt alone at a party. Blaise was the classic extrovert, gaining energy from being around others...from the carefree playfulness of alcohol-induced interaction.

She'd always enjoyed social situations...had thought she couldn't live without them. She'd even felt for a time that Dolfe was being unfair asking her to change.

Tears ran down her cheeks and Blaise sniffled. She'd tried to hide her resentment from him, but he'd seen it. Dolfe was a trained investigator and a brilliant man. He'd known she was chafing at the restrictions he placed on her. Not verbally, but just by his wanting to spend time with her alone and away from her friends.

Looking back, Blaise realized he hadn't pressed or insisted. That his requests for her time weren't unreasonable. That she'd driven him away.

She blinked, her chest tightening under the knowledge. She'd never admitted it to herself before. It had been so much easier to blame him.

But she'd known.

It was why she'd been depressed, she suddenly realized. She'd thrown away the best thing that had ever happened to her for a pretty bauble...a useless sparkling jewel.

She was an idiot.

More shouting. And it was coming closer—

heading her way. Blaise swore. Why couldn't she just have five minutes alone?

A woman ran along the water's edge, her bare feet splashing and splatting against the wet, compacted sand. She was breathing hard...no Blaise realized...she was sobbing. And she kept looking back over her shoulder.

A dozen yards away a man followed, his stride unhurried and aggressive. His silence and determined pursuit seemed oddly ominous and Blaise shivered. He looked to be a young man, with black hair that shone in the glow of a moon freshly extricated from the cloud cover. He wore a Hawaiian shirt that should have looked silly, but on his sturdy, lithe frame it somehow didn't.

The woman wore a gauzy halter dress; its frothy skirt clutched in one hand as she ran. She limped severely and Blaise saw a glossy darkness above one knee that could have been blood.

She frowned. Her gaze sliding speculatively toward the man. Had he hurt her?

Blaise started to stand, pushing to her feet just as a massive wave crashed onto the shore. The surge was louder than it should have been, edged in a sharp retort Blaise couldn't miss from her hours at the shooting range with Dolfe.

Her head snapped up and, for an instant she couldn't see the woman. Then the water rushed away from the shore and she saw the tumbling limbs, the swirling froth of the woman's skirt.

She was lying face down in the surf, her long, golden hair floating around her like gilded seaweed.

Blaise made a soft sound and her hand flew to her mouth, her eyes widening. Her gaze slid slowly along the beach. The man had stopped, his face obscured in shadow as the moon skittered behind a cloud. But he was looking right at Blaise. She could feel his hostile regard like a greasy touch against her skin. His hands were down at his sides, but as she watched in horror, one of them started to lift. She had no trouble recognizing the shape of a pistol gripped in his hand.

Blaise straightened, moved onto the balls of her feet, and dropped her shoes.

She shook her head, backing away as the gun came up, focusing on her. Then she did the only thing she could, fearing it wouldn't be nearly enough.

She turned around and started to run.

3

I like big butts and I cannot lie...

Dolfe's head jerked off the pillow, groggy from an unusually deep sleep. His heart pounded as he reached over and shut off the phone, cursing Blaise. The ringtone had been her idea. Smiling that heart-stopping smile of hers, she'd told Dolfe that it would remind him of her every time it rang. Dolfe silently berated himself for not changing it to something mature and soothing.

She'd been right. The tone did remind him of her...the velvet feel of her skin...the sensual tang of her delicious scent.

God knew he didn't need any more reminders of Blaise. Her essence was infused in every fabric in his home. Her presence saturated every cell of his existence. A battered paperback behind the sofa cushions...a bottle of siren red nail polish shoved to the back of his medicine cabinet.

She was everywhere.

Dolfe had thought breaking up with her would be enough to exorcize her from his life.

What an idiot he'd been.

He opened his eyes and squinted at the clock. Three flippin' AM. He groaned, flopping back to the pillow, and closed his eyes, determined to ignore whoever the asswipe was who thought it was a good idea to call him in the middle of the night.

For a brief, enticing moment he thought he might be able to do it. Go back to sleep. His muscles softened...his thoughts clouded... He took a deep breath, expelling it softly...

I like big butts and I cannot lie...

Dolfe growled his frustration and grabbed the cell, stabbing at the button to answer it. "This better be good."

Silence met his less than friendly greeting.

No. That wasn't entirely right. If he listened carefully, he could hear breathing, soft and staccato. "Who's there?"

A tiny squeak. Panic swirled through Dolfe. "Blaise? Is that you? I'm sorry, honey. You woke me up. What's wrong?" He didn't know how he knew it was her. He just did, in that intuitive, age-old way of lovers who'd been, even for a short time, entirely in tune with each other.

"He killed her."

The simple statement, thick with tears, ripped through whatever grogginess Dolfe might still be feeling and tore him from the bed. He was reaching for his jeans even as he spoke again. "Who killed who, honey. Tell me you're all right. Let's start with that. I need to know right now that you're okay."

She pulled air into her lungs in a shaky breath. "I'm okay. But..." Another squeak, "He saw me, Dolfe. He's coming after me."

Dolfe scrubbed a hand over his face. "Okay, honey, listen to me. Get someplace public. A busy restaurant or something. Sit down at a table facing the door and wait for me. Watch for me. I can be there in minutes. Just tell me where you are."

A soft sob, the sound of the phone dropping, crashing against something.

Dolfe's guts heaved into his throat. "Blaise!"

No response. "Blaise! Talk to me, honey!"

Nothing.

Dolfe paced his room, the jeans forgotten in his hand as his mind struggled to decide next steps. Finally, he disconnected and dialed the number of someone he knew could help.

Detective Brita Muldane answered on the second ring, sounding as if she'd been up for hours. It also sounded as if her mouth was full. "Hebbo?"

"Brita, it's Dolfe. I need your help."

A brief silence and then, "What is it, Dolfe? I'm

on duty in thirty minutes. I'm just scarfing down some toast and then I need to feed the dogs and..."

"Blaise is in danger."

Another silence. Dolfe heard Brita's canine pack lamenting their empty stomachs in the background. "Where is she?" He listened to the jingle of keys and Brita's voice became slightly breathy as she walked. She was already on the move.

"I don't know. Can you send a car to her apartment? Then I need you to trace the call she just made. I'm going to start with her favorite clubs. It will take too long to search them all but I don't know where else to start."

A car door slammed. "No. I'll get your cousins to take the clubs. I need you to go to her place. You'll know better if anything looks wrong there. I'll meet you there in a few...after I call Alf."

Alf Honeybun was Dolfe's cousin and a member of a super-secret organization of the government. His connections and resources often came in handy. Alf would be able to trace Blaise's call faster and with less red tape than Brita would.

"Yeah," Dolfe agreed. "That's good. Thanks, Brita."

Dolfe disconnected and dragged his jeans on, grabbing the shirt he'd worn the day before off the back of a chair and yanking it on. The shirt was wrinkled and smudged with blood from a shaving incident, but Dolfe couldn't think of anything at that moment but getting to the woman he loved.

Nothing else mattered. Not until he held her in his arms again. And assured himself that she was safe.

Fifteen minutes of ridiculously dangerous driving later, Dolfe parked his Jeep Cherokee illegally in front of Blaise's apartment complex and pushed through the glass front doors. The doorman straightened away from his desk and lifted a hand in greeting, recognizing Dolfe. "Mornin' Mr. Honeybun. You're around early."

Dolfe forced himself to stop and greet the older man. "Barney. Have you seen Ms. Runa today?"

The gray-haired man frowned, his pink cheeks puffing up above a thick, handlebar mustache as he appeared to give Dolfe's question some thought.

Dolfe fidgeted impatiently, his gaze sliding to the stairs.

"No, I don't believe I have, sir. I haven't seen her since yesterday morning. She was climbing into a cab with the King of three-pointers." The doorman grinned shaking his head. "Man that guy could shoot long range. It was a sad day when he was cut from the roster."

Dolfe frowned. Dugald Richards was Blaise's

good friend. Blaise had scoffed at Dolfe's jealousy of the man when they'd first started dating, insisting that the two of them had been friends *forever* and that they were like brother and sister.

The only problem was, Dolfe had seen the way the former basketball star looked at Blaise and he didn't look at her like he should be looking at a sister. "Okay, thanks, Barney. Do you think you could call up there for me?"

The man looked surprised but nodded. "Sure, Mr. Honeybun. I'd be happy to." He moved behind his desk and pressed the number for Blaise's apartment, number 301. It rang several times before he hung up. "She's not there."

Dolfe nodded, heading for the stairs.

Barney stood up. "Sir?"

Dolfe slammed his palm flat against the stairwell door, gritting his teeth. He forced himself to turn back, feeling every tick of the clock like a blow to his frontal lobe. "I'm worried about her, Barney. I think she's in trouble. Can you let me into her place?"

The older man scratched his head. "Don't you have a key?"

Dolfe expelled a breath. "We broke up."

Barney shook his head. "Then I don't see how…"

The exterior doors opened, letting a brisk, late December breeze inside that ruffled the thick white hair on Barney's head.

Brita strode in like she owned the place, flashing

her badge. "Detective Brita Muldane, IPD. I need access to Blaise Runa's apartment please."

Barney's small, gray eyes widened and his mouth opened beneath the heavy 'stache. He glanced at Dolfe before reaching for his master key and jerking his head toward the elevator. "I'll have to let you in, Detective."

Brita inclined her head. "That's fine."

Dolfe shoved the stairwell door open, too restless to ride the elevator sedately upward. "I'll meet you up there, Brit."

She didn't even bother to respond, no doubt knowing, from years of experience dealing with Honeybuns, that it would be a wasted effort to try to stop him.

He took the stairs two at a time and burst from the stairwell on the third floor. First he examined Blaise's door and found it locked. It didn't appear to have been tampered with. He walked the hallway, finding nothing to indicate that violence or a scuffle had occurred in the pristine space.

The elevator doors dinged and opened and Brita strode out, catching his gaze.

"Nothing," he reported.

Dolfe fidgeted restlessly as the old doorman hobbled toward apartment 301 and, moving like molasses on a cold day, fumbled with the key until his thick, gnarled fingers finally fitted it into the jagged hole of the lock.

Dolfe skimmed past him as soon as the door opened, leaving Brita to dismiss the elderly doorman. He moved quickly through the living room, peering into the kitchen, and hurried to the apartment's only bedroom. Shoving the door open, Dolfe sucked in a breath.

Brita came up behind him; her Glock held low in both hands. She peered past his shoulder and made a small sound of surprise, lifting her gun. "Stand back, Dolfe."

He glared down at her. "Not a chance." He took a step inside the room and crouched down, pulling a discarded sweater off the floor and lifting it to his nose. Blaise's perfume, a warm and spicy scent that was uniquely hers, rolled over him.

He was vaguely aware of Brita moving through the room, stepping carefully over the clothing and shoes that were strewn all over the floor. Finally, she put her gun away and looked at Dolfe. "This room has been tossed."

Dolfe's gaze rose to hers, burning with the tears he was holding back. "Nah, this is just the way she leaves it when she's packing a suitcase."

Blaise pressed closer to the darkened doorway and crouched down, trying to make her profile as small as possible. She hadn't seen her pursuer for a while, but that didn't mean anything. In the two hours since she'd witnessed the shooting, he'd taken on several forms, with several dark, angry faces. Blaise didn't know if she was being paranoid. She didn't think she was.

The burly Cuban who'd caught her eye when she'd been in the phone booth had been moving directly toward her. And she'd seen the flash of a silver pistol in the street light when his coat had blown back.

It was ninety flippin' degrees in Miami, Blaise mused. There was only one reason you'd be wearing a coat in that kind of heat. And it wasn't a good one.

The man she'd seen on the beach had moved like someone who was used to having all the power. He looked like someone who expected life to go his way, and when it didn't, he dealt out punishment... and death apparently...like he was serving up a Mojito.

Nothing special. Tasty and necessary. Sucks to be you.

Blaise shuddered and wrapped her arms around her knees, lowering her head to rest on them. She thought of Dolfe and guilt turned her stomach to acid. He'd be so worried about her. And when he found out she was gone...beyond his protective reach... Blaise sniffled and blinked back tears.

She'd call him as soon as she could.

"You there, move along. There's no squatting here."

She jerked upright, her heart racing. She'd been so absorbed in thoughts of Dolfe she hadn't heard him walking up. Blaise lowered her head, avoiding his sharp, brown gaze. "Sorry," she murmured, walking quickly away.

"Hey?"

Blaise moved faster. She couldn't trust anybody. It would be just her luck to run up against somebody who was friends with the killer.

Heavy footsteps pounded along the sidewalk and Blaise started to run. She only made it a few steps before a big hand wrapped around her arm, jerking her to a stop.

She struggled, giving a little scream before the man wrapped his arm around her waist and tugged her close. He was soft in the middle and smelled like sofrito and *Cristal* beer, but he was powerful. "You're in trouble?"

She shook her head, struggling to get free.

"Honey, you're much too elegant to be running around barefoot in South Miami Beach at four in the morning. You're running from someone. Who?"

Blaise sighed and gave up struggling. It wasn't

getting her anywhere anyway. "Please, just let me go. I'm not in trouble. I just got lost."

He loosened his grip and stepped cautiously back, looking like he was ready to grab her again if necessary. He reached into his shirt pocket with two fingers and she flinched. He stopped and lifted a hand in reassurance. "I'm just pulling out my badge." He held it out for her to see. "I'm an investigator with the MBPD."

Blaise was torn between joy and terror at the news that he was a cop. She eyed the badge and made a decision. "My purse was stolen and I can't get back to my hotel."

The cop had a fleshy face that made him look older, but Blaise suspected he was probably only in his thirties. Young he might be, but he had old eyes. His speculative brown gaze, deep-set under heavy black eyebrows, held hers unflinchingly. Apparently, he was stubborn too. She tried a smile to soften him up and he finally sighed, offering her his hand. "I'm Jorge Lopez. I only want to help."

Blaise believed him. Unfortunately, she'd learned enough about the way business was transacted in Miami to know that she couldn't trust anybody. Dugald had told her that Cuban gangs had people everywhere, including with the police. She settled on a compromise. "Then can you call me a cab? I need to get back to my hotel."

He reached into his pocket. "I'll take you. Which hotel are you staying at?"

Blaise thought fast, trying to remember a hotel down the beach from hers. A name finally popped into her head. She'd noticed it when walking the beach with Dugald when they'd first arrived. "The Grand Palm."

Jorge pulled a set of keys out of his pocket and touched her arm. "Come on. My car's right over here."

Blaise's nerves twisted under the idea of getting into a car with a man she didn't know, but she quickly weighed her options and realized he was the safest one.

Not to mention the thought of the big suite Dugald had reserved for them, with the huge shower and soft, comfy bed. Once she was rested and fed, maybe Dugald could help her come up with a way out of her current mess.

Fifteen minutes later Jorge Lopez pulled his ancient, pumpkin orange Charger up to the wide front doors of the Grand Palm. A soft breeze rustled through the portico, sending the potted Hibiscus trees fluttering on either side of the white doors. As Jorge put the car into Park, the doors opened and a porter in a dark blue uniform hustled down the stairs, ready to assist with luggage.

Blaise grasped the handle of the door, turning to Jorge. "Thank you for giving me a ride."

"I'll come up with you and make sure your room is safe." His dark eyes fixed on her face, assessing her reaction.

She shook her head. "I'll be fine now. My friend is up there."

Jorge watched her a moment longer. "Are you sure?"

She wrenched the door open and it groaned loudly, the heavy door suddenly shifting from her fingers as the porter took it from her and offered her a hand out. She climbed out and turned back, leaning down to look inside the car. He was still looking at her like he knew she was hiding something. "Thanks again."

She stood on the sidewalk and watched the big car pull out of the circular drive and turn onto Ocean drive.

"Can I help you in some way, miss?"

She turned to the porter and gave him a tired smile. "I'm fine, thanks. I'm just going to take a walk down the beach."

But as soon as the man disappeared back into the hotel, Blaise realized she didn't want to go back out there alone. Despite the comforting roar and crash of the waves on the beach in the distance, the memory of the man lifting the gun as she struggled through deep sand to get away suddenly gripped her lungs, buckling her knees.

She dropped onto a bench and doubled over,

nausea blooming in her belly. What had she gotten herself into? She thought of Dolfe, wondering if he was panicked looking for her. And then she thought of Dugald. She needed to get back to her hotel so she could enlist his help. He would know what to do. They needed to go to the police and then she needed to get out of Miami.

But more importantly, then she could let Dolfe know she was safe. She scrubbed tears off her cheeks and stood up. Looking from the road to the beach, Blaise frowned. Her hotel was down the beach about a quarter mile. If she walked, she'd be exposed again. What if she was spotted on the road? But worse, what if they found her on the beach, alone and virtually helpless?

Blaise looked toward the Grand Palm. She would ask to use the phone and call Dugald. She'd just say someone stole her purse.

Her purse!

She must have dropped the small, sparkly clutch when she released her shoes to run. She'd reacted instinctively, out of fear, and her instincts had told her to get rid of anything that might slow her down and run.

What if the murderer had found her purse? He would know who she was, maybe even be able to track her to the Crestview Empress Hotel where she and Dugald were staying.

Blaise wrapped her arms around her middle and

thought quickly. She couldn't go back there. But she needed to go somewhere.

She looked again at the white doors. She'd call Dugald and have him bring her things. She would stay at the Grand Palm until they could get out of Miami Beach.

Feeling better for having a plan, Blaise hobbled up the steps toward the door, her feet sore and her legs immeasurably tired from her night's adventures. When the doors opened again, Blaise smiled at the porter. "Can I use the phone? I have an emergency."

The man's dark eyes slipped over her, hesitating briefly on her dirty, bare feet. "Of course, miss. If you'll follow me, you can use the phone in the Concierge's office."

Blaise preceded him through the door, her gaze sliding quickly around the large, plant-filled lobby. The room encompassed the entire depth of the hotel, opening out through a series of floor to ceiling glass doors onto the beach beyond. The ocean-side doors were open, allowing the soft, tangy scent of the sea to filter through and rustle the brightly flowered succulents and potted citrus trees dotting the lobby. High above her head, perched on the branches of an enormous coconut palm in the center of the space, vibrantly colored parrots squawked and called hello to the room at large.

The porter strode quickly toward a small office located to the left of the front doors, the glass wall sporting the word *Concierge* in tall, gold letters. He opened the door and flipped the switch to illuminate a small lamp, casting the room in gentle amber light.

"Would you like something to drink? A glass of water, perhaps?"

Though the man's dark eyes seemed ever-watchful and curious, his manner toward her was polite and kind. Blaise reacted to that kindness so viscerally it threatened to take her legs out from under her. Sudden, hot tears flooded her eyes as she shook her head. "I'll just be a minute. I need to call a friend."

He inclined his head and stepped out of the room, closing the door quietly behind him. Blaise sat down behind the desk and picked up the phone, quickly dialing her friend's cell.

Dugald answered on the second ring. He didn't sound as if he'd been sleeping. "Hello?"

"Dug, it's me, Blaise."

"Oh my god, girl! I've been so worried. What the heck happened to you?"

Blaise rested her head on her hand, suddenly too tired to hold it up. "It's a really long story. Can you come get me?"

"Of course. Where are you?"

Blaise heard voices in the lobby and looked up, her weary gaze looking for the source. A dark-haired man wearing a polo shirt and dark slacks was leaning against the reservation desk, talking on the phone.

"Blaise? Are you still there?"

Blaise's hand tightened on the phone. Her pressure spiked.

"Blaise?"

"He's here."

As if he'd felt her watching him, the man's head turned slowly in her direction.

4

*B*laise dropped the phone and dove toward the ground, scurrying under the desk. She made herself as small as possible and took deep breaths to keep from hyperventilating. Blaise strained to hear the man's voice, praying he would return to his conversation and forget about the concierge's office.

But she wasn't going to be that lucky. A moment later the door opened and the sounds of a slowly awakening hotel filtered into the little office. From where she hid, she could just make out a long, narrow shadow across the carpeting. Blaise bit her lip, trying to keep from screaming as the tension ratcheted.

"Sir?"

Blaise twitched and closed her eyes, recognizing the porter's voice.

"Was there someone in this office, Estefan?"

"Yes sir, a woman. She was using the phone."

Silence pulsed as Blaise imagined both men looking into the empty office.

"Did you see where she went?"

"I'm sorry, Mr. Blanchette, I didn't."

"Find her. I need to speak with her."

"Yes, sir."

Blaise's stomach twisted with fear. She needed to get out of that hotel.

The shadow held for a moment longer and then shifted. Blaise thought he was starting to move away and then a tortured shriek exploded on the air and she jumped, banging her head on the top of the desk.

It was a parrot, just a parrot! Blaise took a deep breath and held it, trying to still her pounding heart.

The shadow hesitated, lengthened.

Blaise silently cursed herself. Had he heard her?

"Mr. Blanchette, you have a call."

The woman who approached on heels that clacked loudly against the tiled lobby floor had a warm, husky voice. Blaise wondered if it was the brunette he'd been speaking to at the front desk.

"Who is it?"

"A Jorge Lopez."

"Did he say what he wanted?"

"No, sir. Only that it was important."

Blaise held her breath as the shadow on the rug stilled. seeming to hesitate.

"Shall I tell him you'll call him back?"

"No. I'll take the call. Thanks, Millicent."

Blaise waited until his shadow left the room and then darted out from behind the desk, straightening away from it and reaching to shut off the lamp. She stood to the side of the door, chewing her bottom lip as she watched him, trying to figure out what to do.

He stood in front of the admissions desk, speaking on the phone. There was no way she could get past him and out the door. His gaze kept drifting to the Concierge's office, dark and suspicious.

Just when she thought she might have to make a run for it, the front doors opened and a large, noisy group came through. They were obviously drunk and thankfully very distracting. The group of six men and four women moved past the office, toward the elevators, stumbling and laughing loudly, plastic cups of something clutched in their hands.

The man's dark, feral gaze slid toward the group and away, dismissing them as he continued his conversation.

Blaise put her head down and slipped into the group, moving quickly toward the hallway with the bank of elevators. They barely gave her a look as she scampered along beside them and then peeled off to run along the hall toward the *Exit* door at the end.

"Hey, lady. Where ya goin'?" The drunken shout

sent a wave of cold horror skidding through her and Blaise ran faster, her heart pounding in her chest. She plunged through the door at the end of the hall and found herself standing on a sand-covered sidewalk at the edge of the beach.

In the near distance the surf pounded and sighed against the sand, the salty tang of water bringing a sudden, terrifying sense of déjà vu to spur her into a run. She dove behind a fringe of palms just as the door she'd exited through opened, casting a wide swath of white light over the walkway.

Blaise flung herself to her belly in the warm sand and went very still, thankful for the drone of the surf to cover the strident sifting of breath from her lungs. Terror clutched at her chest, tightening it painfully.

She lifted her head only high enough to find him, a long, dark form standing in the doorway. He was framed by the soft, white light of the hallway behind him and his gaze slipped along the sand, stopping at the copse of trees in the exact spot where she hid. Blaise clamped her lips tight on a whimper.

She could almost feel his gaze against her skin. Like fire ants biting her quivering flesh. Blaise's muscles tightened, preparing for flight. He stepped away from the door, letting it clang shut behind him.

Blaise's toes dug into the sand. Her fingertips tightened against the ground. She was going to bolt, run for all she was worth.

Somebody laughed, a natural, husky sound that

throbbed on the early morning air. The man stopped, his gaze sliding to a couple of women gliding toward him with feline grace. They swayed together, arms tangled in a maze of affectionate familiarity, gazes locked.

His scrutiny slipped back toward Blaise and she could almost hear him considering whether he should go for her.

But in the end, he merely lifted a hand, index finger stretched in her direction like a gun and turned back into the hotel.

Blaise didn't wait to see if he came back out. She was on her feet, kicking up sand at the edge of the beach, her calves screaming from a long night of overuse.

Listening to his cell phone ring, Dolfe paced Blaise's living room while Brita searched for information on where she might have gone. He prayed the owner of the club where Blaise worked was still there, though the bar had closed an hour earlier.

He'd just about given up when Tyrese Miller answered.

"Yo."

"Ty, it's Dolfe Honeybun."

"Hey, my man. What up?"

"I'm looking for Blaise. I was hoping you could tell me where she was."

A beat of silence throbbed through the line before Tyrese responded. "She didn't tell you?"

Dolfe's heart thudded against his chest. "Tell me what?"

Tyrese swore. "I'm sorry, man. Forget I said anything. She's not here right now."

"Ty, tell me where she is."

"Sorry, man. I ain't gettin' in the middle o' dis."

"We broke up, Ty. I know she's with Richards. I know they left town. I just need to find out where. She called me a while ago and she's in trouble."

Tyrese whistled through his teeth. "Sum bitch. She didn't tell me where they were goin', man. Only that she needed to get away for a while. She took two weeks, man. Two whole, frickin' weeks. I don't know how I'm gonna get through Christmas without my most popular waitress."

Acid filled Dolfe's belly as his hopes were dashed. "If you hear from her..."

"I'll get as much information as I can and call ya. You got my word on that, man."

"Thanks, Ty."

Dolfe disconnected and closed his eyes, scrubbing a hand over them. He was shocked to find the hand shaking.

"No luck finding her?" Brita asked. She strolled

into the living room, her stride quick and her hands empty.

"No. Tyrese says she's gone for a couple of weeks."

Brita frowned. "That sounds like a serious vacation. I hope she's not in Europe."

Dolfe couldn't agree more. If Blaise was that far from him she'd have to hold on a really long time until he got to her. He slipped his phone into his pocket and started for the door.

"Where are you going?"

"To Blaise's best friend's house. She tells Suzie everything."

Brita followed him to the door. "Wouldn't it be faster to call her?"

Dolfe ducked into the elevator while Brita closed the door to Blaise's apartment and hurried after him. "It would be, except she won't answer her phone. She works until two AM and once she falls asleep she's dead to the world."

Brita skipped down the steps right behind Dolfe, her voice breathy as she struggled to keep up. "I'm guessing she won't open her door either then."

He turned to his friend, a mean grin sitting uncomfortably on his face. "Oh, she'll answer her door. And if she doesn't, I'll break it down."

Brita's stare heated the back of his neck. Dolfe picked up another small rock and chucked it at the closed window a couple of floors above their heads. "I can feel your judgy attitude, Muldane."

"I'm just making sure you don't do something stupid, Honeybun."

He chucked a third rock at the glass, his fingers working another one from his palm. "I'm not going to do anything stupid."

She made a rude noise behind him. "You will. You won't be able to help yourself. You're a Honeybun."

He chucked a fourth rock at the glass and was happy to see the room-darkening drapes twitch slightly. A second later a small, pale face appeared between the curtains, a leopard patterned eye mask adorning her forehead.

Suzie Whotsnoggin glared down at him, but she unlocked her window and shoved it up. "What the heck, Dolfe?"

"I need to come up, Suz. Blaise is in trouble."

Her glare turned to a frown. "I'm not fallin' for that, Honeybun. You just leave that poor woman alone. She's trying to cope with the breakup. You're only makin' it harder on her."

He lifted his hands in surrender. "I'm not giving you a story, Suz. Blaise called me and told me she's in trouble. She dropped the phone before she told me what was going on."

Still the woman above him hesitated. So Dolfe used his ace in the hole. Pointing to Brita he said, "You've met Brita Muldane? Indianapolis *Police* Detective Muldane?"

Brita gave the other woman a little finger wave. "We need to speak to you Miss Whats..." She glanced at Dolfe, lifting one fine, blonde eyebrow.

"Whotsnoggin."

"Miss Whatsnoggin."

Suzie Whatsnoggin's lips twisted as her small teeth worried the bottom one. Then she nodded. "Okay, but this had better not be another attempt to get me to talk to Blaise for you. What you did you did, Dolfe. You need to own it."

"I promise."

A second later the front door buzzed and Dolfe and Brita pushed through. They climbed a wide staircase covered in stained, musty smelling carpet and headed for the open door at the end of the hall on the third floor.

They found Suzie dumping coffee into a machine in the kitchen. She was wearing yellow silk boxers with big red hearts on them and a white tank top. Her eye mask was lying on the counter next to the coffee maker.

She yawned widely and hit the start button on the coffee maker. "Tell me about Blaise. How do you know she's in trouble?"

He told her what he'd told Tyrese. "She said

she'd seen something and a man was after her." He fixed her with a stern look. "She called me looking for help, Suz. I need to go to her. But I don't know where she is."

The woman chewed her bottom lip with indecision.

Dolfe's temper flared. "We don't have much time! Blaise could be in danger right now." What could the woman be struggling with? Did she not believe him? Then it hit him. "I know she's with Dugald Richards."

Suz moved to the coffee maker and poured coffee into three mugs, handing one to Brita and setting one on the square, two-person table in front of Dolfe. "And you promise me that's not why you're here." Her bright blue gaze lifted to his and he saw anger there, crisp and hot.

He sighed, lowering his gaze. "I'm sorry I hurt her, Suz. You have no idea how sorry I am. But I can't take that back now and I promise you on my mother's life that I'm not lying to you. Blaise called me and she's in trouble."

A phone rang into the silence that followed. Suz picked up a small cell phone covered in pink bling and answered it. "'Lo?" She listened for a moment and her pretty gaze widened. "You sure?"

Dolfe saw stars as Suzie's gaze slid to his, filled with fear. "He's here right now. He told me pretty much the same thing. Did she sound like she was hurt?"

He took a step forward but Suz shook her head and held up a hand to stop him. "Okay, thanks Dug. I'll tell him."

"That's Richards?" Dolfe tried to grab the phone.

Suz dipped her shoulder to avoid his grasp and stepped away, disconnecting. "He says Blaise didn't come back to the hotel last night. Really early this morning she called him too, but before he could find out where she was she dropped the phone." The woman's slim legs wobbled and she placed a small hand on the glossy surface of the wood table. Slowly her gaze skimmed to his. "You need to go, Dolfe. Dugald needs your help. He's already bought you a ticket. It's waiting at the airport for you."

Dolfe nodded, turning for the door. "Where is she?"

Suzie's bright eyes filled with tears. "Miami Beach."

He started to run. Her strident, worry-infused voice called after him. "Find her, Dolfe. I'm counting on you."

He didn't respond, didn't want to take the time even to thank Brita. He'd do that later. After he found Blaise and brought her home safe.

5

It was hard to see her reflection in the stained and cracked mirror. The yellow illumination from the light fixture in the ceiling didn't offer much help, but Blaise thought she'd achieved the effect she wanted.

A pair of large, brown eyes stared back at her from the cloudy mirror, framed in thick black lashes that were completely natural. Gone were the long, glittery party girl lashes and eyeliner. Also gone was the enormous afro Blaise was so proud of. In its place was a smooth blonde wig shaped in a chin-length bob. She couldn't believe how different she looked with just those two changes.

She wished she could see the clothes too. Comfortable boyfriend jeans skimmed her slim ankles and a loose, white oversized man's shirt was tied at her waist, a plain black t-shirt beneath it. Flat white sneakers completed the homespun outfit. She hoped she looked like a tourist, hapless and non-threatening.

Except for her eyes, which were wide with fear and something else that made Blaise proud.

Determination.

She might be on the run for her life but she was no dang victim. She'd learned a thing or two from Dolfe over the months they'd been together. She'd learned how to keep a low profile and pass unnoticed while hiding in plain sight, cloaked in anonymity. Something party girl Blaise had never thought she'd crave.

She didn't need Dolfe or anyone else to tell her that going up against a wealthy local businessman was a dangerous proposition. If Mr. Blanchette at the Grand Palm was a favorite city benefactor, the cops would take his word over Blaise's in a heartbeat. And she would quickly find herself in even deeper trouble than she already was, exposed and alone, with no resources and nobody to turn to. As long as Blaise was operating under her own steam she was okay because she *did* have resources. She just needed to figure out how to get to them.

Thoughts of Dolfe brought new brightness to the enormous, waif eyes in the mirror. Blaise'd had to hock the diamond earrings he'd given her for their six month anniversary to get the stuff she needed. But she promised herself she'd go back to that seedy pawn shop as soon as she fixed the current mess she was in and get the earrings back.

They were the last thing she had that tied her to Dolfe and it would kill her to lose them.

Blaise nodded at her reflection and turned away from the mirror, heading for the door.

Her plan was simple. Get to Dugald and hide out in the hotel while he used his Miami connections to get her to safety. Hopefully, they could find out who the man at the Grand Palm was and if he was under the protection of the local police. She thought of the cop she'd met. He'd seemed like someone she could trust. But then he'd called the Grand Palm and turned the killer on to her. She wouldn't make the mistake of trusting someone she didn't know again.

Blaise slipped her oversized sunglasses on and slunk through the door, emerging into a crowded shop filled with touristy stuff like dogs made out of seashells, cheap beaded purses and tee shirts that read, *Ho-Ho-Hotel Miami Beach.* With a picture of a palm tree draped in multi-colored lights. A reindeer reclined beneath the palm tree wearing sunglasses and holding a tall, fruity drink in one hoof.

Blaise grinned, wishing she could buy Dolfe one of the shirts. He'd love it.

She emerged from the trinket shop into bright sunlight and glanced up and down the beach. Unlike the night before, the deep, yellow sand was full of people.

Families with small children took advantage of the seasonal savings and lower temps to enjoy the beaches and entertainments. Locals wearing glossy tracksuits walked the beaches with sun-darkened skin. Young professionals ran with barking, happy dogs along the water line.

Blaise envied them all their carefree enjoyment of Miami Beach. She thought of all her plans for the vacation. Lazing around the pool all day, drinking icy Mojitos and dancing at frenzied clubs all night. It had been a lovely dream.

She sighed and pulled off her shoes, heading for the surf. She'd walk along the waterline, surrounded by people, to the Crestview Empress Hotel. She thought it was about a mile down the beach from where she was. Hopefully, she'd recognize it from the beach side. She'd only been out there once with Dugald, shortly after they'd arrived. She remembered an extended patio filled with tables and edged in curving palm trees with twinkling white lights.

An hour later, calves screaming and shirt damp with sweat, Blaise saw the Empress. She said a silent prayer and started toward the patio. Blaise realized it must be lunch time because the tables were about half full. As she approached, the scent of spicy Cuban cooking filled the air.

Her mouth watered. Realizing she hadn't eaten anything since lunch the day before, Blaise decided she'd get room service as soon as she got to the room. The thought made her smile.

A big hand clamped around her arm. "Miss Runa?"

Blaise jerked, gasping and tried to pull away from the grip. It only tightened until it was painful. The man holding her stood at eye level, which made him just under six feet tall, and wore aviator shaped sunglasses with mirrored surfaces that cast the sparkling lights of the palms back at her when she looked at him.

"Let go of me. That's not my name." She tried again to jerk her arm free.

His full mouth turned up in a mean smile, which creased his fleshy, brown cheeks. "Mr. Blanchette wishes to speak to you."

Blaise jerked her arm and gave a little shriek. "Let me go!" The man leaned close, his thick fingers digging painfully into her flesh. He spoke softly against her ear, his spicy breath leaving behind a moist film on her skin. "If you don't want your friend Dugald to end up floating face down in the surf you'll shut up and come with me quietly."

Blaise stilled, gooseflesh popping along her arms. She swallowed hard. "Don't hurt him. I'll come quietly."

The man inclined his chin. "This way. I have a car waiting nearby."

Dolfe barely noticed the people swirling around him as he departed the plane at Miami International airport. They were just smears of color as he strode quickly past, his gaze in the distance searching for a recognizable face.

He'd made the call while waiting to get on the plane in Indianapolis and he'd been relieved when his old friend had answered. It had been a long time since Dolfe had spoken to his college pal, nearly as long since he'd learned Jo had left the Miami Dade Police department to become a private investigator, with a specialty in serial crime.

Dolfe was hoping Jo could use years' worth of experience climbing around in the underbelly of Miami and Miami Beach to help him find Blaise more quickly.

The terminal was busy, frothing with travelers and the people there to see them off and greet their arrival. Dolfe scanned hundreds of bobbing and moving faces in search of Jo. He was starting to worry that he'd been stood up when a familiar voice called his name.

"Honeybun!"

He turned and saw the wide brown eyes and tousled mop of golden-brown hair he remembered so well. Dolfe lifted a hand in greeting and headed in Jo's direction. The crowd parted before his determined stride. Or maybe it was the worried scowl on his face that inspired them all to get out of his way. Dolfe didn't care either way. He just wanted to get out of that airport and start looking for Blaise.

He pulled his friend into a hug, surprised by the pleasurable jolt of seeing Jo again. "Jumpin' Jo! How the heck are you?"

Joanna Granger beamed up at him from well below his chin. "I haven't heard that one for a while." She embraced Dolfe, smacking him hard on the back before stepping away. "It does bring back memories." She scanned him a look. "So...I see you're still freakishly tall."

His grin widened. "And you're still cartoonishly short."

Her caramel colored cheeks dimpled prettily. "I'll have you know I've almost reached five whole feet." She turned toward the glass doors leading outside.

Dolfe chuckled, picking up the duffle bag he'd dropped to the floor to hug her. "Oh yeah? How'd you manage that?"

"Yoga." Jo told him as they stepped outside. "Stretched me right out."

Moisture-clogged heat punched into him as he followed her outside. Even at barely nine AM the temps were already in the low eighties and humid enough to wilt Dolfe's button-down shirt. His Midwest winter-acclimated frame immediately sprouted copious amounts of sweat to try to deal with the shock of it. "Another ten years of yoga and you might achieve normal size."

She laughed the soft, husky laugh he remembered all too well. "Shut up, Honeybun."

He groaned as she stopped beside a lime-green clown car. "Please tell me this isn't yours."

Her brown eyes sparkled suspiciously. "The Smart Car is very eco-friendly." The locks clicked open and JJ slipped inside. "Come on, Mr. Cranky. We're burning daylight."

He opened the tiny door and bent down to peer inside. "Should I strap my bag to the roof?"

"Get in, funny guy."

Dolfe flung his duffle into the small, cluttered back compartment and curled himself into a near fetal position, pinching his long form into the passenger side seat. He felt like he was sitting on the ground.

JJ patted his knee, which was only inches from his face. "Ready?"

"Don't think I won't get even for this."

She laughed gaily and backed from her spot, heading for the exit. Her smile slid away and she quickly became all business. "I thought we'd start with her hotel." She glanced at Dolfe. "Blaise's."

He nodded, pulling out the photo of him and Blaise he'd taken from her apartment. "This is Blaise."

JJ studied it for a moment and then handed it back. "She's gorgeous."

Something about the way she said it had Dolfe's gaze sliding to her face. Her expression was blank. Unreadable. "Dugald Richards didn't know what had happened to her but I want to question him anyway. He probably knows more than he realizes."

JJ nodded. "We'll question everyone she interacted with last night. I ran a trace on her phone and found the last location." She skimmed him a look. "It was on the beach down from their hotel. The battery was missing."

Dolfe's pulse picked up as fear razored through him. "She might have dropped it."

"And then took the battery out?"

He suddenly found it hard to swallow. "There has to be an explanation. Maybe somebody stole it."

"And removed the battery, why?"

Dolfe stared straight ahead, barely seeing the pastel and palm quaintness of the area as they sped toward Miami Beach. His heart pounded painfully and his palms were sweaty. "You think somebody took her down?" Acid swirled in his gut as he forced himself to ask the question.

JJ's dark gaze briefly fixed on him. "I'm paid to think that, Honeybun. It's pretty much my default. Just ignore me and hold onto that hope you're clutching like a binkie. We're gonna find your girl."

Dolfe frowned as she made the turn onto a short,

winding drive leading to the Crestview Empress Hotel. He noticed his friend hadn't speculated on what kind of shape Blaise would be in when they found her.

That's what was really worrying Dolfe.

He sighed. "Tell me."

She glanced his way. "What?"

"Whatever it is that you're trying so hard not to tell me."

JJ frowned. "It's this case I've been working."

Pain shot up Dolfe's thigh and he realized he was squeezing it in anticipation of what she was about to tell him. "Go on."

"Something's going on in Miami Beach. Young women have been disappearing. Just dropping off the face of the earth. It's really got me stumped." Her gaze slid to his. "This morning a jogger found a woman's body."

Dolfe's head jerked around. Terror tore through his gut like a bullet. "It's not Blaise!"

Her gaze widened and she shook her head. "Oh god, I'm sorry. No. It isn't her. I didn't mean to imply..."

He sucked air slowly into his lungs, forcing his rock hard muscles to unclench. "Don't scare me like that, JJ."

She pulled the clown car into a parking spot and killed the engine. Heat flared in the car like a ravenous beast skulking in the shadows waiting to attack. Despite the temperature of the closed vehicle, Dolfe realized he couldn't move. Terror had locked him into place. "Do you think it's a serial?"

JJ reached for the handle to her door. "I didn't until we found the body. Now I'm not sure."

He frowned. "What did you think was happening?"

She expelled a weary breath. "MBPD has kept a clamp on this so I shouldn't tell you..."

"But you're going to, right JJ?" He glared at her, the tension returning to his neck and shoulders at the possibility that she might refuse to answer.

"You have to keep this close, Dolfe. If they found out that I told you..."

"Really? You think you need to tell me that?"

Sighing, she opened her car door but made no move to get out. "Sex slavery. The streets are buzzing with it but nobody knows any specifics. All we know is that pretty women...tourists mostly...are disappearing from clubs, parties and bars. One tourist from Iowa disappeared one morning while she was jogging on the beach. Nobody's seen anything. Nobody has any clue how it's happening."

"And until this morning you found no bodies?"

"None."

"How was she killed? The woman on the beach?"

"Shot. Twice. A through and through in the left thigh and the fatal shot to the back of the head. SIG P226 9MM."

"A cop's gun," Dolfe said.

She frowned. "You don't even want to go there, Honeybun."

Dolfe scrubbed a hand over his chin and it came away wet from sweat. He opened his door and a warm breeze drifted through the tiny car. "If Blaise saw it happen…"

JJ nodded. "Yeah. She's got not one killer but a whole organization after her."

"Son of a…"

"Let's not get ahead of ourselves. We have no proof that that's what happened. Hopefully, we'll find her and discover it was all a big misunderstanding."

Dolfe wanted to believe that. Unfortunately he was a realist and, *realistically*, the chances of Blaise calling both him and Richards in a panic and then turning up and telling them both it was just a misunderstanding were less than nil.

His gut was telling him she was in deep trouble and running for her life.

His gut was also telling him that he needed about a gallon of sodium bicarbonate.

6

*B*laise wasn't surprised when the big black SUV pulled up to the Grand Palm, but she *was* a little surprised when the car drove around to the side and entered an underground parking garage marked for service deliveries.

Since the moment she'd been thrown into the back seat by the guy wearing mirrored sunglasses, the driver of the big car had studiously avoided glancing in the mirror, almost as if he knew the knowledge of what she looked like would be a liability at some later time. The thought brought an icy chill down Blaise's spine, making her shiver.

Mr. Mirrored Sunglasses glanced her way. His thick lips spread in a smile. "Someone walk on your grave?"

She glowered at him but stayed silent. During the five minutes it had taken them to travel from the

Empress to the Palm, Blaise had tried to take stock of her situation and had come to the horrifying revelation that she was in deep trouble. Nobody knew where she was. Dolfe didn't even realize she'd left Indianapolis. Her only friend in the area was probably in just as much trouble as she was—all because of her need to be alone and brood about Dolfe.

Looking back she realized how stupid and careless she'd been. She should never have been on that beach by herself so late at night. After all, look what had happened to that other poor woman. Blaise swallowed hard. Although, she *could* make the argument that if the dead woman *had* actually been by herself she wouldn't be dead.

Blaise got a flicker of understanding for how frustrated Dolfe must have been with her. Her careless inattention to mundane details like safety had nearly driven him crazy.

Turned out he'd had a point.

The Escalade stopped beside a wide, gray metal service elevator.

Mr. Mirrored Sunglasses grabbed her wrist, speaking to the driver. "Stay here in case he wants to move them.

Them.

Blaise had clung to the hope that they didn't really have Dugald. She'd hoped they were just using the threat of him to keep her in line.

Mirrored Sunglasses dragged her across the seats

with him as he exited and slammed the heavy door shut behind her. Blaise stared into the driver's side window, willing him to look her in the eyes. Darned if she was gonna let him pretend she didn't exist. She had no idea if the man returned her determined gaze or not. The windows were tinted nearly black.

Mirrored Sunglasses pulled her toward the elevator. He punched the button and the doors slid open with a shrill whine that made her wince. She silently berated herself for looking weak in front of the thug. After all that had happened to her over the last twenty-four hours, her nerves were shot. Blaise straightened her shoulders, tipping her chin up in defiance. Whatever happened she would deal with it.

She wasn't going down without a fight. She owed that to the poor woman on the beach.

Mirrored Sunglasses pressed the button for the penthouse suite.

Blaise thought it was strange that the service elevator went that high, but then decided the man in the penthouse must use the elevator to sneak into his home when he didn't feel like being friendly.

Or, maybe he used it to hide activities and people he didn't want to be noticed. Blaise suppressed another shiver.

The elevator stopped and the doors slid open, the whine dulled by the lush carpets and thick grass wallpaper of a private entry. Her kidnapper dragged her out of the elevator and knocked politely on the mahogany door directly across.

A moment later the door opened and a man with a flat, suntanned face looked out at them. His hostile hazel gaze slid in Blaise's direction. "That her?"

Mirrored Sunglasses nodded.

Flat Face stepped back. "Mr. Blanchette is in the library."

Any small trace of hope Blaise had nursed over her destination died under those words. She was in the home of the scary, dark-eyed killer from the beach. Hustled in the back way. Unseen.

She was well and truly alone. If she was going to survive her current mess it would be up to her to find a way.

Her mouth watered as a wave of nausea took her. And then she was being yanked forward again and, despite her determination to be strong, Blaise's eyes stung under tears of real fear.

"What do you mean he isn't answering?" Dolfe growled at the wide-eyed desk clerk. "I just spoke to him this morning. Mr. Richards assured me he'd stay in the room and wait for me."

The clerk's heavily made-up eyes cranked open another notch as Dolfe pressed closer. She swallowed hard, her long fingers caressing the glossy wood of the registration desk as if thankful it stood between them. "I'm sorry, sir. Maybe he's in the shower. Or out on the balcony."

"Tell me which room he's in and I'll go up there." Dolfe glowered menacingly at the poor girl, hoping to terrify her into going against hotel policy.

But she was made of sterner stuff than that. She shook her head, displacing the fine, mousy brown strands of her stringy hair. "I can't do that, sir. It's against ho..."

"Hotel policy, you already said that," Dolfe grumbled. "About a thousand times."

JJ put her hand on his arm, pressing it subtly. Dolfe's frown deepened but he allowed her to push in front of him. The movement was meant to reassure the frazzled clerk. JJ as a calm, reasonable buffer against the raving lunatic with wild, green eyes.

JJ smiled at the clerk. "Is Bobby around, Jessica?"

The girl's hazel gaze slid toward Dolfe as if reassuring herself that he wasn't going to come at her again.

He forced a smile onto his face that felt like metal over plastic and she blinked, leaning away from him in response.

Epic fail on the smile.

"He's in his office, just wrapping up a meeting."

JJ's smile was much less intimidating than Dolfe's. "If I could I'd like to speak with him."

The clerk nodded and turned away. "I'll call him."

A moment later she hung up and gave JJ a strained smile. "Bobby will be right up."

"Thanks!" JJ grabbed Dolfe's arm and dragged him away from the registration desk. Dolfe decided he'd probably imagined the relieved sigh behind them. "Who's Bobby?"

"Manager."

"The manager of the most expensive hotel in Miami Beach is on a first name basis with his employees?"

JJ looked amused. "He's a bit eccentric."

"Jo Jo, my darling!"

"Gird your loins," she murmured to Dolfe before turning toward the booming voice. Dolfe turned too, his gaze looking for a well-dressed, elegant proprietor in a dark suit and red tie.

But the man who hurried, chuckling happily, toward JJ was about as far from the image as he could be.

"Bobby" was a large man with white-blond hair that was cut short and stood up from his head in nearly translucent spokes. His broad face was shiny, his cheeks rosy red, the color too uniform and bright to be real.

Dolfe's suspicion that the man wore makeup was

confirmed when he stopped a foot away from them, well inside Dolfe's comfort zone, and grabbed JJ's hands, pulling them to his puffy lips. He fluttered long lashes that were thick with mascara and danced their hands between them. "You look just delightful today, *ma chérie*. Are those new capris?"

JJ laughed. "I've worn them a time or two. But I don't think you've seen them. How's that recommendation I gave you working out? Did you take my advice?"

The enormous, spiky head snapped back as Bobby bellowed happily. "Delightful. We enjoyed the club very much. I'm seeing him again tonight."

JJ's eyes sparkled. "Good. I knew you two would hit it off."

Bobby's bright, heavily-made-up gaze swung toward Dolfe and widened. "My, my. Who's your friend?"

Dolfe fought the urge to take a step back as the man moved in, way too close, and grabbed his hand, pumping it between soft and meaty paws. "I'm Bobby and you're..." He laughed. "Delicious."

"This is my old college buddy, Dolfe Honeybun."

Bobby's gaze sparkled with good humor. "Perfect name. Just perfect."

JJ laughed with him.

Dolfe glared at her. "I...we...need your help, Bobby."

The big man moved even closer, though Dolfe

wasn't exactly sure how. They'd already been close enough to have sex. "Anything for you, *ma chérie*." He winked at JJ. "And of course you, *mon ami*."

The man spoke French like he was from Arkansas. But Dolfe liked him despite the fact that he was a close talker and Dolfe instinctively mistrusted close talkers. There was no good reason to get that close to a virtual stranger. Unless of course you no longer wanted to be strangers.

"I'm looking fo..." Dolfe started to explain but JJ talked over him.

"Dolfe came to see Dugald Richards." She paused, her gaze widening slightly as if trying to portray some hidden meaning. "But Richards isn't answering his phone and Dolfe is worried."

Bobby's puffy lips opened on an "Ahhh." The meaning of which was unclear to Dolfe. "Le sigh," the big man went on. He smiled at Dolfe. "All of the good ones are either straight or taken." Glancing toward the desk, the manager pointed toward the clerk Dolfe had harassed. "You, Tiffany Crystal, give this lovely man the key to Dugald Richards' room. Toot suite." Bobby winked at Dolfe, reaching to smooth a big hand over Dolfe's shoulder. "If you ever want a change, *mon amour*. You know where to find me." He placed his fleshy lips over Dolfe's, making a small sucking noise as he kissed him. Dolfe didn't even have time to react before the man pulled away and lifted a hand. "I'm off. Much to do. Ta, Jo Jo. I'll talk to you later."

Dolfe stood for a beat with his mouth open, his eyes bulging out of his head. He watched Bobby stride quickly away as if he'd forgotten they even existed.

"What's the matter, Honeybun. You look like you've never been kissed by a man before." JJ's voice wobbled suspiciously.

Dolfe blinked and looked at her. "I can't believe you did that to me."

She shrugged, her eyes sparkling. "I told you to gird your loins." She waved the key card in front of his face and started toward the elevators.

Dolfe shook off his shock and followed. "I didn't realize you were being literal. Besides, you should have told me to gird my lips."

JJ's throaty laugh trailed back to him. "It's a small price to pay for this, isn't it?" She handed him the keycard.

Dolfe frowned at the card as the elevator doors slid closed. He guessed it was. Probably. Well...maybe.

Then he remembered why they were there and he decided it definitely was. In fact, he decided he'd have gone a lot further with the manager of the Crestview Empress if it would bring Blaise safely back to him.

7

He stood before a crackling gas fire, a real luxury given the temps outside the elegant penthouse apartment. His hands rested on the mantel above the fire, the long, tapered fingers looking like they hadn't done any serious work for years.

Blaise couldn't help thinking about one of them pulling the trigger on the beach the night before. The man was apparently accustomed to deadly if not manual labor.

He turned as Blaise was dragged into the room, his dark gaze flashing with interest as it skimmed her from the top of her head to her sensible, tourist shoes.

"Well done. I'm a little surprised my men were able to spot you in that outfit."

Blaise dredged up years of party girl indifference and allowed it to paint her expression. "I don't know who you think I am, mister, but I don't appreciate being dragged off the beach and manhandled. I have rights you know."

His handsome features held amusement. "Nice try, Miss Runa. But it isn't gonna sell. You see, if you don't want somebody to know who you are you really shouldn't drop your purse on the beach." His amused gaze slid to a small, glass table to Blaise's right. Her pretty, beaded party purse lay on the table, a dusting of sand spoiling its pristine beauty.

She blinked in an effort to mask her surprise. "That's a pretty bag. Whose is it?"

The man laughed, glancing at Mr. Mirrored Sunglasses, he said. "Leave us, Bent. Stay outside in case I need you to clean blood off the floor."

Despite her best intentions, Blaise could feel her eyes widening.

Mirrored Sunglasses' lips twitched as he inclined his head. "Sir."

Blaise kept her eyes on the tall, elegant man standing before the fireplace as the man named Bent walked from the room, closing the door quietly behind him. Her unwelcoming host had shoved his hands into the pockets of perfectly tailored blue-gray slacks and cocked his head, studying her with a practiced eye.

She would have given a year's tips to know what

he was thinking. But she wasn't going to ask. "I'm serious, mister. You've got the wrong girl. I just got here last night from Ohio. I've never seen that purse before and you and I have never met." Her voice trailed off on a slightly desperate squeak. Blaise cleared her throat, stubbornly holding his gaze.

When he smiled, his almond-shaped eyes narrowed slightly. "You are delicious. I couldn't really get a good look at you on the beach last night." He glided closer, one hand coming up to skim along her jawline.

She couldn't believe his arrogance. He wasn't even trying to pretend he didn't murder that girl.

Blaise jerked her head away but didn't anticipate his next move. He grabbed the strands of her blonde wig and yanked it off her head.

His smile widened. "Much better. With a little makeup..."

"I don't know what you want from me but I'm not going to stand here and let you examine me like a prize hog."

His laughter rolled across her nerves like thunder on the edge of a storm, alarming and terrible with promise. "More like a rare and exquisite swan, actually. But you might as well get used to it. I was just going get rid of you, but now that I've seen you..." A smooth fingertip trailed down her throat and lower.

Blaise tried to jerk away but he grasped her arm

in an impossibly strong grip. In the blink of an eye his handsome face turned cold, icy with rage. "You are no longer free, beautiful swan. You're mine to do with as I choose. You might as well get used to the idea. It will be your reality for the rest of your very short life."

Fear clawed at her throat, tamping down on her ability to draw breath. Blaise tried to hold onto her bravado but terror made it hard. "I have friends. You can't just do what you want to me." She only hoped she wasn't lying.

The cold mask slipped away and a warm, almost comforting smile took its place.

Blaise realized at that moment that she was dealing with a crazy man. One who seemed to have unlimited wealth and power.

"The only friend you want right now is me, beautiful swan." He cocked his head. "Maybe I'll give you the chance to make me your friend." The grin widened, turned lecherous. "It only makes good business sense. I need to know the full value of my asset don't I?"

Blaise kicked him on the knee and it buckled with a sharp creak. He bellowed in pain and swung his fist, clipping her on the side of the head as she tried to turn away. Stars burst before her eyes but Blaise shoved him away and stumbled toward the balcony. Behind her, a shout went up but she didn't slow or turn as the library door slammed open.

Grabbing hold of the handle to the French door, Blaise wrenched it open, plunging through. She fell against the balcony railing and looked down, her eyes nearly going crossed at how far away the ground was.

Vertigo swam through her head, making her vision blur. But Blaise didn't have a choice. It was either jump, aiming for the densely populated pool far below, or become a sex slave to a genuinely crazy *hombre*.

She'd rather die.

As the door behind her crashed outward, Blaise lifted her leg over the railing and leaned out over space. Big, hard hands grabbed for her as she let go of the balustrade, shoving it away as she started to fall.

～

"Wherever he is, Dugald didn't leave his room willingly," Dolfe told JJ. Richards's room had looked like there'd been an MMA fight in it and, beneath the broken furniture and glass, all of Dugald's things seemed to still be in the room. Including his cell phone and wallet. "I guess young women aren't the only ones being abducted in Miami Beach, Jo."

JJ frowned, her small hands tightening on the steering wheel, but didn't comment.

Dolfe fidgeted in the tiny car seat, feeling like a caged animal surrounded by black leather and glass. "You have to have some CIs who might know what happened to Blaise. Surely somebody saw something."

JJ glanced at him, her pretty face a study in patience. He'd been haranguing her about Blaise since they returned to the ridiculous car. "I talked to all of my informants right after you called me from Indy. They're asking around but so far nobody's turned up anything."

"That's impossible. Blaise looks like a runway model for Vogue. She doesn't exactly blend in, Jo. How much do you trust these informants?"

She made a turn onto Washington Avenue and parked in front of a large white building with a rounded front and yacht-shaped extensions. The words, *Miami Beach Police*, adorned the wall above the entrance in bright blue letters.

Killing the engine, JJ finally turned to him. "First of all, if Blaise was taken from an empty beach at night then it's highly likely nobody saw anything. Secondly, I trust my CIs to take care of themselves and not much else. If Blaise is running from or has been taken by someone with a lot of power and connections, even my most dependable informant might plead ignorance rather than risk dying for fifty measly bucks."

Dolfe's fingers drummed against his thighs.

"Then I need a list of every wealthy, powerful jerk you think is dirty in this town. I'll personally visit every one of them."

She shook her head. "I'm hoping it won't come to that. I have a friend with MBPD. Maybe he has information I don't. Or can get it."

Dolfe glanced at the strangely shaped building. "That's why we're here?"

She nodded. "Come on."

He was standing in a corner cubicle, eyeing a computer monitor and talking to another officer. He looked up as they approached, his gaze narrowing when he saw Dolfe. The cop extended his hand to JJ. "Jo, how's it going?"

She shook his hand, jerking her head toward Dolfe. "Pez, this is Dolfe Honeybun. An old friend. He's here looking for his girlfriend. He thinks she's in trouble." She turned to Dolfe. "Honeybun, this is Detective Lopez, Criminal Investigations Unit."

The man lifted heavy, nearly black eyebrows and offered his hand to Dolfe. "Nice to meet ya, Honeybun. How can I help?"

"As Jo said, my girlfriend Blaise is missing. I think she witnessed something..." Dolfe told the cop. "I believe she's on the run and I'm trying to find her before the other guy does."

Lopez and JJ shared a look that made Dolfe's gut twist in alarm. "What?"

JJ shook her head. "I was hoping you might have heard something on the streets," she told Lopez.

"About the disappearing girls?"

JJ flashed Dolfe a guilty look. "Yeah. You heard about the woman's body that turned up on the beach?"

The cop's gaze narrowed. "You don't think it was..."

"It wasn't Blaise," Dolfe interrupted with more heat than was warranted. Even the thought of Blaise being murdered and left alone on a deserted beach was enough to make him crazy.

Lopez seemed to take Dolfe's hostility in stride. "I was off duty but the Captain called me back to help them canvass and interview. It was a huge dead end. Coroner put TOD at approximately one in the morning. Nobody saw anything. Everybody was either asleep or in the bars. The nearest hotel has a line of palms around the patio which blocked that part of the beach."

"Any evidence of a scuffle or a third person being on the scene?" Dolfe asked gruffly.

Lopez shook his head. "I'm sure you can imagine how hard it is to identify disruption in the sand, Honeybun. Especially where the surf comes up."

JJ touched Dolfe's arm in support or warning. He

wasn't sure which. "Have they ID'd the dead girl yet?"

"Samantha Rocklee," Lopez responded with a frown. "Twenty-four years old." He shook his head, clearly disgusted. "She was here with a bunch of her girlfriends from Wisconsin. Her friends said she met a guy at a bar in Little Havana and left with him. But none of them could give us a clear description of the guy."

JJ expelled a breath. She glanced at Dolfe. "Same story every time. The guy's like a ghost. Nobody knows what he looks like...or the descriptions we get are completely different."

"Maybe he *is* a ghost," Dolfe offered.

Lopez snorted before he realized Dolfe was serious. "That's not helpful, Honeybun."

"I don't mean ghost as in *Boo*! I mean ghost as in military training."

JJ lifted her eyebrows. "It's an angle we haven't considered." She nodded. "I'll look into that. In the meantime, have you heard anything about a tall, slender black woman with a big afro and delicate features," JJ asked Lopez.

"She has a smart mouth," Dolfe added brusquely.

Lopez's brown gaze widened. "Do you have a picture?"

Dolfe dug the photo out of his shirt pocket and handed it to Lopez.

The cop stared hard at it for a moment and then shook his head. "Well, I'll be damned. I can do you one better. I met her myself. Early this morning."

Dolfe stepped closer, fisting his hands in an effort to keep from grabbing the guy and trying to shake the information out of him. "Where? When?"

Lopez shook his head. "I knew she was in trouble. She was huddling in a doorway on my street and she was barefoot, looked panicked. She told me she'd been robbed and just needed a ride to her hotel." Jorge tensed as Dolfe moved into his space, fists clenched with rage.

"Why the hell didn't you help her?"

Lopez held up a hand in warning. "Back off, man. I helped her as much as she'd let me. I gave her a ride back to her hotel."

Dolfe's throat vibrated on a growl before he could stop himself. "She never showed up at her hotel. Her traveling companion called me this morning...worried about her. And now he's disappeared too."

Lopez swore. "I had a feeling she wasn't telling me the truth about the hotel." He caught Dolfe's eye, a warning glint in his gaze. "I'll tell you everything I know, but you need to take a deep breath right now."

JJ touched his arm. "Dolfe..."

His jaw hurt. Dolfe realized he was clenching it. He stepped away from Lopez and lifted his hands in surrender. "Sorry. I'm wound kind of tight right now."

Lopez snorted. "Really? I hadn't noticed."

Dolfe's teeth creaked. Impatience had him stepping tcward Lopez again. "Where did you take her?"

"The Grand Palm. She insisted she had a room there."

8

The Grand Palm was a huge glass and metal sculpture rising from the sandy soil along South Miami Beach with wide, triangular pillars under a flaring three-sided portico in the front. Balconies lined the entire façade, their undersides painted pristine white and forming a type of architectural daisy chain that marked the division between floors.

JJ parked the clown car in a palm-shaded lot and Dolfe was out, striding toward the entrance before she killed the engine.

She ran to catch up with him. "You need to let me do the talking, Dolfe. You're too emotional. You'll scare the stuffing out of everybody."

He kept walking and didn't respond.

"Dolfe..."

"I'll let you talk, JJ."

She sighed loudly, knowing he'd agreed to something entirely different from what she'd suggested. "Just try not to send them running for the panic button."

"I promise I'll try."

The porter smiled as they approached and opened his mouth to welcome them. Dolfe pushed past as the man opened the door, rudely ignoring him.

He could hear JJ thanking the man and then the click of her heels as she crossed the veined, white marble floor behind him.

Dolfe headed for the tidy teak registration desk and the tall, attractive brunette managing it. She smiled as he approached, showing a mouth full of perfect white teeth to go with her flawless hair and excellent features.

Dolfe inclined his head in mute greeting. "Can you check to see if a woman named Blaise Runa checked in here this morning, please?"

The woman's smile held but became tight around the edges. "I'm sorry, sir I can't do that. It's against hotel policy."

Dolfe leaned over the counter. "I think maybe you need to do it anyway."

The woman blinked and reared back in surprise. "I...ah..."

JJ joined him at the counter, smiling widely. "Hi, Millicent." JJ showed the woman her Investigator's license, neatly laminated and driver's license-sized. "I don't know if you remember me. I was here last week about the disappearance of the woman on the tenth floor."

Millicent slid a look toward Dolfe before returning JJ's smile. "Jo Granger?"

"That's right! You have a great memory, Millicent."

The woman shrugged but her cheeks pinkened with pleasure. "It's part of my job. How can I help *you*, Ms. Granger?"

Dolfe didn't miss the slight emphasis. He'd already pissed one of them off. Great. He pulled Blaise's picture from his pocket.

"We're looking for this woman. She's missing as of last night. A witness placed her at this hotel this morning. We just want to verify that she checked into the Grand Palm. Her name is Blaise Runa."

With a final swing of a hostile gaze in Dolfe's direction, Millicent glanced at the picture, shaking her head. "I haven't seen her before but she might have come in while I was on my break." The registration clerk punched a few keys on the computer and shook her head. "Nobody by that name has registered."

"Try Suzie Whotsnoggin," Dolfe suggested.

Millicent frowned. "Can you spell that?"

Dolfe frowned. "I don't have any idea. Just like it sounds I guess."

He could see that the ever-efficient Millicent would have rather eaten worms than help him, but to her credit she made a visible effort to shove her irritation back and comply.

Probably because JJ was sucking up to her big time.

A moment later Millicent shook her dark head. "No. I'm sorry. I've tried several spellings of Whot-snoggin and there's nobody here by that name either."

"Okay. Thank you for trying, Millicent."

"Sure," she chirped. "Anytime." She looked Dolfe in the eye. "Have a great day."

"Yeah, you too," he mumbled.

JJ fell into step beside him as he strode to the door. She was practically running to keep up with his much longer strides. "Do you think she was telling the truth?" he asked his friend.

"Why would she lie?"

"I don't know, but Lopez said he dropped Blaise off here this morning."

"He also said he didn't see her go inside."

When they reached the door Dolfe shoved it open. The porter had scurried over to ask a man and a woman disembarking from a taxi if they needed help with their bags.

Which gave him an idea. "Hold up a minute, JJ."

They waited until the porter ushered the couple through the door and then Dolfe approached him, pulling out Blaise's picture again. "I'm sorry to bother you but..." He held the picture out to the man. "Have you seen this woman?"

The porter took the picture and glanced at it, smiling. "I have. It was very early this morning. Right after I came on duty." He handed the picture back to Dolfe. "I remember her because she was such a pretty thing. And she was barefoot." He shook his head. "Poor thing seemed upset. Wanted to use the phone."

Dolfe's heart started to pound. "The phone? She went inside?"

The man nodded. "I showed her to the Concierge's office. Pandora doesn't start until ten in the morning," the man told them by way of explanation.

Dolfe slipped the photo back into his shirt pocket. "Can you show me?"

The porter led them back inside and across the gray-veined marble floor to a glass-fronted office. The mahogany tinted door was open. It had a brass plate on it that read, *Concierge*.

An elegant older woman wearing cat-eye glasses sat behind the desk. She looked up as the doorman walked through the door, smiling at him. "Good morning, Estefan."

The porter inclined his head in greeting. "Pandora, these nice people wanted to know about that poor girl who asked to use the phone this morning."

The concierge frowned. "Oh? Are you from the police?"

JJ opened her mouth to respond but Dolfe beat her to it. "Yes. I'm Detective Honeybun and this is Detective Granger." He could feel JJ's gaze scalding him but he didn't look at her. He pulled Blaise's picture out and laid it on the woman's desk. "Have you seen this woman? She went missing last night."

The woman named Pandora picked up the photo and her gaze lifted to him, apparently noticing that he was in the picture too. "You know the victim, Detective?"

"I do."

"Isn't that a conflict of interest?"

"That's why I'm here, ma'am, JJ said helpfully, stepping between Dolfe and the concierge as if blocking the woman's view would make Dolfe disappear. "Have you seen the woman in that photo?"

Pandora shook her head. "I don't come in until ten o'clock. Esteban told me he left her in my office around four in the morning." She handed the photo back to JJ.

Dolfe stepped around his friend. "Why were you and the porter discussing Ms. Runa?"

The woman blinked in surprise. "Oh, well there's nothing sinister in that, Detective. When I came into my office the phone was lying on the floor under my desk. Esteban heard me asking Millicent about it and he told me what he'd done."

Dolfe looked at JJ. "Millicent?"

Pandora nodded. "Yes. Have you spoken to her?"

JJ fixed her features into a stern expression. "We have. But she didn't mention the incident. Do you think you could ask Millicent to join us here? I'd like to ask her some follow-up questions."

The Concierge stood. "Of course. I'll go get her."

Blaise screamed as rough hands hauled her back. She kicked and punched and bit at the hand that covered her mouth.

Bent grunted in pain as her teeth broke the skin and punched her in the side.

Agony razored through her. A bright, sharp ache sliced into her lower back and Blaise's knees buckled. She struggled to draw breath as the pain ricocheted through her, blossoming outward.

Her mind screamed for her to fight back, but misery had turned her arms and legs to jelly. Still, as Bent tucked his arms under hers and started to lift, Blaise snapped her head back, connecting hard with his nose. She knew she'd broken it because she heard a very satisfying cracking sound.

The man roared his outrage and dropped her.

Blaise's head hit something hard on the way down and it snapped her head forward. Fresh torture, dull and hot swept down her spine.

Something connected with her hip and she yelped as she was launched sideways.

Bent kicked her again and Blaise tried to scrabble beneath the glass-topped table she'd slammed into.

Then somebody yelled and Bent stopped, turning away and growling a response.

Blaise was vaguely aware of voices, angry and urgent, and then something bit her arm. A quick pinch, before the sky above started to dim, the fluffy clouds spreading over it and cloaking her world in a cotton haze that slowly darkened to black.

The lovely and recalcitrant Millicent stood in the doorway, hands clasped before her, and gave Dolfe stone face.

He'd been questioning her for fifteen minutes and had all but accused her of kidnapping Blaise herself. A small portion of his mind, the professional part, told him he was blowing it. He was letting his emotions rule and it was getting in the way of the investigation.

He'd expelled JJ moments earlier because she kept telling him to calm down. She'd been too much like his conscience and his patience had snapped.

Deep down he knew she was right, which was probably why she'd annoyed him so much. But his heart was a giant, bleeding hole in his chest and all he wanted to do was smash and tear.

He scrubbed a hand over his face and tried again, forcing his tone to moderate. "Look, Millicent. I'm sorry to come at you so strong. But I'll be honest with you. The woman I love is missing and I have reason to believe she's in a lot of danger. I can't help feeling like I'm racing the clock. I'm asking...no, scratch that...I'm begging you to help me find her." Dolfe was embarrassed by the unsteady quality of his voice as he battled emotions that were too big to contain. He was appalled by the moisture stinging his eyes. But he'd made a conscious decision to open himself up to the woman...to let her see the raw emotions driving him so she'd understand. What emerged was just about as raw as it came.

He knew the honesty had paid off when her gaze softened. She unfolded her hands and moved sideways, sliding gracefully into the leather chair beside the door. He forced himself to wait while she stared at her nails, appearing to consider carefully what she was about to say.

Finally, she looked up and he could see the doubt in her eyes. But she didn't back down from it. "There was a woman." When Dolfe nodded encouragement, she hurried to clarify. "I never saw her."

He forced himself to sit on the edge of the desk and wait.

"I was working the desk early this morning. Mr.

Blanchette was at the desk too. He was speaking to a client on the phone when Estefan came through the lobby and told me he'd let a young woman use Pandora's office and phone."

She hesitated, took a deep breath, and then went on. "Mr. Blanchette seemed startled. He ended his phone conversation and walked over here. He stood in the doorway, just staring into this office a moment before he motioned Estefan over and asked him about the woman."

Dolfe frowned. "He didn't come inside?"

She shook her head.

"Was the young woman here?"

Two vertical lines deepened between Millicent's perfectly shaped brows. "No. That's what was strange. The office was empty but he just stood there. He seemed deep in thought. In fact, I called out to him several times before he heard me. He had another phone call. I think I asked him if he wanted me to take a message. I'm not sure. He looked at me like he wasn't really listening at first, but then he turned and walked toward the front desk."

"He took the call?"

She nodded.

"Was it unusual for him to take calls at the front desk?"

"Oh no. He's a hands-on type manager. Most days he's out here on the floor more than he's in his office."

Dolfe inclined his head. "Then what happened?"

"His call was short and when he hung up he turned toward a group of clients who were laughing and talking loudly over by the elevators. One of them shouted something and Mr. Blanchette started running in their direction." Her brows lowered. "I remember thinking he was acting very strangely. Maybe it was something Officer Lopez said."

Dolfe's head jerked up, he straightened away from the desk. "Officer Lopez?"

"Yes. That was the second phone call. The one that drew him away from Pandora's office."

Dolfe swore. He hurried into the lobby, heading for JJ, who was talking on her cell phone, her small hands flying around as she spoke.

9

*B*laise struggled to wake up. Her mind felt like it was mired under layers of sticky, black tar. Her limbs were heavy, unresponsive. She kept her eyes closed and concentrated on moving her fingers and then her toes. Opening her eyes, she tried to lift her arm and gasped. Her arm and shoulder were sore.

She lay still for a moment, trying to remember what had happened. Nothing came to her. She looked around the room and realized she wasn't at home and that surprised and worried her because she didn't know where she was. She shoved the covers back and started to get up, only to be jerked back by something around her wrist.

Her gaze whipped around and she made a small sound of fear when she saw the fur-covered handcuff holding her to the headboard.

"What in the world?"

The door across the room opened. A tall, handsome man with cold blue eyes came into the room carrying a tray. He was limping slightly. The man smiled broadly. "You're awake. Wonderful. He set the tray down on the bedside table and sat down on the edge of the bed.

Blaise tried to scoot away from him but the cuff severely limited her range of motion. "Where am I?"

He reached toward her face and she flinched. He halted, smiling softly. "You don't remember the accident?"

Blaise shook her head. "What accident?"

He sighed, reaching to pull the covers up. "You were in a car accident." He shook his head, running a long, elegant finger along her arm. "I blame myself. I should have driven you instead of asking you to meet me here."

Blaise frowned. "Car accident?" That would explain the soreness. "I was coming here?"

He nodded, cupping her jaw gently in his hand. "I had to work late and you wanted to see me." He laughed, rubbing his thumb over her cheek. "You're such an impatient lover."

Blaise squirmed uncomfortably. She wasn't sure if it was his words or his touch that made her stomach tighten with disgust. She jerked her captured hand. "Why am I handcuffed?"

He looked at the cuffs like he'd forgotten they

were there. "Oh. I'm so sorry. The doctor prescribed a sedative for you last night and you reacted badly to it, flailing around and writhing on the bed. I didn't want you to hurt yourself." His hand slipped down her throat, threatening to go lower.

Panicking, Blaise jerked the cuff to distract him. "Take it off."

His gaze darkened for a split second but then he smiled tightly. "Of course. You're not a prisoner here, Blaise."

"It sure feels like I am," she murmured.

He reached into the pocket of his slacks and pulled out a key.

"Why can't I remember?" She watched closely as he unlocked the cuffs and released her. Scooting away from him on the bed, Blaise tucked herself into a ball against the headboard and rubbed her wrist.

He looked so sad that it momentarily threw Blaise off. "It hurts me to see you so suspicious, darling."

She shrugged.

Sighing, he stood up. "The doctor told me the drug he gave you might cause some limited amnesia. It will pass." He walked toward the door. "Rest for a while. Later I'll take you out on the yacht." He turned at the door and smiled. "You'd like that, wouldn't you? It's Christmas Eve. I've invited hundreds of my closest friends. It will be good to spend time together without any worries or cares."

He cocked his head, something dangerous sparking his gaze. "Won't it, darling?"

She stared, unmoving until the door closed behind him. Then she jumped up, grinding to a halt with a groan as agony shivered through her. She felt like she'd been beaten with a rolling pin. Blaise breathed through the pain and then hurried toward the door, trying the knob.

It was locked.

~

JJ frowned at him, her arms crossed defensively over her chest. "I have no idea why Jorge would call here. It might not have anything at all to do with this."

Dolfe glared at her. "Come on. You don't really believe that do you?"

She shrugged.

"Then why didn't he tell us about the phone call?"

JJ shook her head. "I don't know. I've known Jorge Lopez for a long time and I trust him. There's got to be something…"

Dolfe walked past her and approached the registration desk. Millicent was with a client and she looked at him nervously as he approached. It was clear she expected him to make a scene. Dolfe had no intention of fulfilling that expectation. He would wait thirty seconds and then he'd go find Blanchette himself.

Millicent dispatched the client quickly and professionally, smiling widely as she handed the man dressed in a wrinkled business suit his key card. "Thank you for visiting the Grand Palm," she told him cheerfully.

The man grabbed the handle of a small black suitcase and lumbered wearily toward the elevators, bag trailing in his wake.

Millicent's cheerful demeanor crashed as she swung her gaze his way. "What?"

"I want to see Blanchette."

She leaned over the counter, lowering her voice. "*Mr.* Blanchette is very busy."

Dolfe leaned in too, until their faces were inches apart. "Unless *Mr.* Blanchette wants me to create a doozy of a scene, he'll get unbusy real fast."

Murmuring Spanish swear words that she probably didn't expect Dolfe to understand, the woman picked up the phone and punched in a number.

Dolfe observed her as she waited for the call to be answered. She looked nervous.

In Dolfe's experience, only people with some-thing to hide got nervous when he asked questions.

She turned away and spoke softly into the phone.

"Jorge said he was worried about Blaise so he

called the manager to tell him she was there and might need help."

Dolfe turned and found JJ looking at him as if she'd been vindicated. But something in her pretty eyes told him she wasn't entirely buying the cop's story. "And you believed him?"

"Why wouldn't I? It makes perfect sense."

"Yes," Dolfe said. "It's very tidy."

JJ frowned.

"Mr. Blanchette is coming down now."

"Down? Down from where?"

"I'll show you to his office," Millicent offered evasively. She spoke to another clerk behind the desk and came around. "Follow me, please."

They followed the woman down a quiet hallway with expensive shops on either side, past a hair and nail salon and a taffy shop. The sweet smell of candy made Dolfe's stomach growl and he realized he hadn't eaten anything all day.

Millicent stopped in front of a closed door with a brass nameplate that read, *Austen Blanchette*. Opening the door, she motioned for them to enter.

Down the hallway an elevator dinged and a tall, dark-haired man in perfectly creased, charcoal gray slacks and a white polo shirt emerged, striding toward them down the hall. Austen Blanchette smiled widely when he saw Dolfe. The man's teeth were so white against his tan and so perfect they didn't look real. He had the well-groomed good looks of a George Hamilton but was a few decades younger.

He took JJ's hand as she introduced herself.

"It's nice to see you again, sir. I don't know if you remember me? I was here a couple of weeks ago about the young woman from Wisconsin?"

"Of course I remember you, Ms. Granger. It's nice to see you again."

As Dolfe gripped his hand, he couldn't shake the feeling that Blanchette was just as much an actor as Hamilton. The hotel manager was a few notches short in the sincerity department.

"I'm so sorry to hear about your girlfriend, Mr. Honeybun. That's very concerning. I'm sure the police have told you that several girls have gone missing lately."

Dolfe released Blanchette's hand. "They have. Blaise isn't one of them, Mr. Blanchette. I'm not leaving Miami Beach until I find her."

Dolfe watched the other man carefully and saw the quick flash of interest in his gaze before he nodded, pasting an appropriately grave expression on his too-handsome face. "I understand. I'll do anything I can to help you find her."

Dolfe allowed himself to be ushered into the office. It was richly appointed but not extravagant in any way. Dark hardwood covered the floor and the walls were painted a soft, creamy yellow. The desk at the center of the space was large and looked to be of the same dark wood as the flooring. It sat at an angle from the door, centered on a rug of a deep red color. A sideboard ran along the back wall, its glossy surface holding nothing more exciting than binders marked with plain white labels proclaiming their contents.

The air held a slight, sweet tobacco smell. Dolfe guessed Cuban cigars.

Blanchette moved around the desk and sat in a black leather chair. He glanced at the door. "Thank you, Millicent. Please close the door when you leave."

She inclined her head and, with a final hard-to-read glance at Dolfe, left the room.

Blanchette shuffled papers. "I'm sorry for the mess. I've been approving requisitions for special supplies all day." He grinned. "We're having our annual Christmas party on the yacht tonight."

Dolfe's eyebrows lifted. "Yacht?"

Blanchette chuckled. "Yes. It's not mine, I assure you. *The Grand Lady* was my predecessor's idea. I hate to admit it because it's a ton of extra work, but the annual holiday parties on the yacht were an inspired idea. They've nearly tripled our holiday profits and are largely responsible for us filling most of our rooms every Christmas."

JJ leaned forward, smiling. "I've been to one of the weekend parties on the *Lady*, Mr. Blanchette. I can attest that it was a wonderful event."

"Please, call me Austen."

She inclined her head in agreement. "Only if you'll call me Jo."

"Short for?"

She flushed prettily. "Joanna."

"A much prettier name than Jo," Blanchette told her with his movie star smile.

"But not very useful when trying to function in a man's world," Jo responded.

He nodded, ceding the point. "Our weekend dance cruises are well attended." He crossed his legs and folded his hands on his thigh. "But I'm sure you didn't come here to talk about *The Grand Lady*."

JJ leaned forward in her chair. "What can you tell us about Ms. Runa, Austen? I understand she was here very early this morning?"

Blanchette shook his head. "Unfortunately I never saw her. When Estefan told me he'd ushered a young woman into the concierge's office I was curious. I don't mind admitting I'm a bit more cautious these days. Such a tragedy, all these sweet, young women disappearing. It has put a pall on the Grand Palm. My staff is extra cautious and none of my female employees walk alone to their cars anymore. Not even during the day." He shook his head. "I hope the police catch whoever's responsible soon."

"Back to this morning," Dolfe pressed. "Your clerk told us you received a call from Jorge Lopez?"

"Yes. That's correct. Officer Lopez wanted to tell

me he'd dropped a woman off at the Palm and that she seemed upset. I promised him I'd find and question her...see if there was anything I could do to help."

"So when Estefan told you he'd put a young woman into the concierge's office..." JJ prompted.

Blanchette's head bobbed once. "I hurried over. But she wasn't there."

"Did you get a description, sir?"

Blanchette shook his head. "I'm afraid I didn't. Only that she seemed troubled."

"Millicent told us you heard something near the elevators and ran that way. What was it, Austen?"

The skin around his eyes tightened for just a blink, but then he gave them a sad smile. "I'm afraid it was nothing. The group of young people was very drunk and rowdy. One of them called out something like, 'Hey lady!'." Blanchette laughed, seeming embarrassed. "I thought maybe it was our distraught young woman."

"But it wasn't?" Dolfe asked.

"No. There was nobody there other than the group of young partiers. And they all climbed into the elevator together, so..." He shrugged. "I'm sorry I couldn't be of more help. I don't like thinking that another pretty young woman might be in danger."

Dolfe stood abruptly, offering Blanchette his hand. "Thank you for your time, sir."

JJ could barely keep up with him as he stalked across the hotel.

"Would you mind telling me why we tore out of there?"

Dolfe pushed through the front entrance and approached Estefan.

The man looked up and smiled as he saw them approach. His welcoming smile slid away when he saw the look on Dolfe's face. "Is something wrong?"

"You told Mr. Blanchette about the woman who used the phone this morning?"

Estefan nodded. "I did. I thought he should know she was in the hotel..."

"Did you describe her?"

The porter's bushy eyebrows lowered thoughtfully. "I...no. I told him a woman had asked to use the phone and she seemed upset so I put her in Pandora's office."

Dolfe reached out and touched the older man on the shoulder. "You're sure?"

"I believe so, yes. Is something wrong?"

Dolfe patted the man's shoulder. "Thank you, Estefan. He reached into his pocket and pulled out his wallet, extracting a twenty. "Have a nice day."

The other man stood with the twenty dollar bill flapping in a soft breeze and stared after Dolfe as he strode away again, clearly confused.

Dolfe was no longer confused. In fact, he finally knew just where to look for Blaise.

JJ followed as he headed for her car, huffing and puffing behind him. Finally, she got a hand on his arm and dragged him to a halt. "Mind telling me what's going on?"

"He's got Blaise."

JJ looked perplexed. "Estefan?"

"Blanchette." Dolfe shrugged off her hand and started walking again.

She frowned. "Look, Dolfe, I know you're upset about Blaise, but you can't just accuse Blanchette based on conjecture..."

Dolfe reached for the door handle, frowning when he found it locked. "It's not conjecture. It's a strong gut feeling combined with the fact that he described Blaise without supposedly having seen her."

JJ shook her head. "Because he assumed she was young? Come on, Dolfe..."

"Young and pretty. She could be coyote ugly as far as he knew. Why would he just assume she's pretty?"

"Because she's obviously missing and all the other girls who came up missing were young and pretty?" JJ crossed her arms over her chest, her expression worried. "Dolfe, you don't know the culture here in Miami Beach...the politics. Blanchette is a well-established feature in the social scene. He's wealthy and connected. His family's money has been a staple of all types of charities for as long as I can remember. People love the man. They love his family. They love the family's dogs for god's sake. Nobody would even consider that Austen Blanchette was involved in a kidnapping." She shook her head. "I have to tell you, I think you're seriously off base on this."

"That kind of makes him the perfect guy to get away with it then, doesn't it?"

She opened her mouth, hesitated, and then closed it again, shaking her head.

"There's a reason you haven't been able to find this guy, JJ. Because you're looking in the wrong place. It's obviously somebody outside your parameters. Blanchette is outside your parameters."

She didn't look convinced. "I'm not going to be able to sell this to my sponsor on the MBPD."

"I understand, JJ. If this is going to be a problem for you, I'll go it alone."

"Honeybun…"

He shook his head. "Don't waste your breath. Blanchette has Blaise and I'm going in to get her."

10

*B*laise tried the French doors to the balcony and found them locked. She wondered if she could break them quietly enough not to draw the attention of whoever stood guard outside the bedroom door. She'd spent the past several minutes with her ear pressed against the door trying to hear what they were saying.

Unfortunately, all she could make out was the gruff rumble of male voices and, occasionally, laughter.

She'd like to know what they were laughing about.

The doors were heavy, well-made, and Blaise couldn't find anything in the room to jimmy them with. The dressers were all empty. The adjacent bathroom had only a couple of towels and some small bottles of shampoo and body wash. It was apparent the man holding her captive had experience and apparently knew what a prisoner might use to escape.

Snippets of her memory had been returning since the man left her alone in the room again. She remembered trying to get away, someone kicking her and the pinch on her arm that had to have been them injecting her with something. That would explain the memory loss.

But the most terrifying thing she remembered was what he'd said about her never being free again.

His threat weighed on her, creating panic.

She had no idea how she was going to get out of that room. But she was darned if she was just gonna give up and let them take her god knew where to be a slave.

"Ain't no slave crap gonna happen to this black girl," she murmured angrily. Her gaze slid around the room, looking for something to use as a weapon. Nothing popped out at her. Even the pictures were hung without glass. She eyed the frames. Maybe...

The door opened and Bent came in, his nose swollen and purple where she'd smashed her head into it. Blaise blinked under the unexpected memory.

The thug glared at her so she smiled just to annoy him.

"Keep grinnin' bitch and I'll give you a nose to match mine."

She let the grin slide away but held his gaze, determined not to appear weak. "You can't keep me here."

Bent threw a garment bag onto the bed. "Really? That's strange. It looks like we are." He flung a plastic bag on top of the garment bag. The smaller bag looked like it contained a shoe box. "Boss wants you to dress up and make yourself pretty. We're leaving for the boat in a couple of hours."

She glanced toward the French doors, where the sun was still high in the sky. "It's a little early to start the party, isn't it?"

Bent headed for the door. He stopped, the edge of the wood door clasped in one big hand and glared at her. Beyond him, Blaise saw another man holding some kind of assault rifle. "There's more than one party gonna happen, bitch." He laughed at her shocked response to his threat and winked before leaving her alone in the room again.

Blaise didn't spend a lot of time fretting over his veiled threats. She was too busy eyeing the hanger he'd just brought into the room.

～

J J drove in silence, a frown darkening her pretty face.

Dolfe barely noticed. His mind was churning over what he'd learned to that point. He had a sudden thought. "The Grand Palm has dance parties on the yacht every Friday night?"

She shook her head. "Saturday nights. They're really popular with the under thirty crowd." She glanced his way. "Why?"

Dolfe thought for a minute. "Was there any pattern in when or how those missing women disappeared?"

JJ chewed her bottom lip thoughtfully. "I'd have to check my records to make sure but I think they all disappeared late in the week."

"Like Friday or Saturday?"

Her gaze swung to his. "What are you implying?"

"I think you know what I'm implying, JJ."

She shook her head, turning into *Lease a Ruin* car rentals. "You can't really believe Blanchette is kidnapping these girls."

"I really can. You have to admit a yacht is a great place to hide someone."

"Then what?"

Dolfe shrugged, reluctant to say what he was thinking because of what it might mean for Blaise.

"Oh my god, Honeybun. You think he's killing them and dumping them at sea?"

He frowned. "I didn't say that. I don't know what he's doing with them. But there's only one way to find out. I'm going to get myself onto that boat to look around."

JJ expelled a breath. "Why are we here?"

Dolfe grinned. "You can't do surveillance from the clown car. You might as well put a sign on your chest that says, *Look at me, I'm spying on you.* This stupid car's too conspicuous."

JJ climbed out. "It's not stupid." She slammed the door, glaring at him over the roof of the tiny car. "You're paying for this rental, Honeybun."

He draped an arm over her shoulders, leading her toward the shack at the back of the lot that was apparently the rental office. "I wouldn't have it any other way, Jumpin' Jo."

J J dropped him at the Marina where *The Grand Lady* was docked. He peered at the sky, noting the lowering sun and realizing he was running out of time. If Blanchette was doing something weird with the kidnapped girls and the yacht was involved, he would need to show up early with his victims so no one would see them arrive.

Dolfe parked his butt on a bench at the edge of a wide swath of Florida grass and watched as caterers and musicians and every other dang thing paraded on and off the *Lady*. He was glad he'd made JJ stop along the way to get what he needed. Pulling the shapeless white cotton jacket from one bag and the covered foil pan from another, Dolfe slipped a few goodies he'd begged, borrowed and stolen from JJ into the pan and covered it again, crimping the edges over the white cardboard top.

Anxious to get on board the yacht, he strode toward the parking lot, where a white van with the logo, *Delicious D'Lights to Go* painted in vibrant colors on its side was parked.

The truck was a hive of frantic activity. Dolfe waited until most of the white-coated workers left and then walked up and smiled at the harried looking woman with the clipboard. She was in the back of the van, checking the contents of each pan of goodies and checking them off on her clipboard. She looked up as Dolfe appeared in the doorway, round blue eyes narrowing suspiciously. "Where'd you get that?"

He glanced at the pan in his hands and gave her his most disarming smile. "I'm from *Camila's* in Miami. Mr. Blanchette requested our famous Cannoli for his special guests tonight."

Realizing Dolfe wasn't one of hers, the red-cheeked woman dismissed him. "Oh. Okay. Don't scare me like that." She patted a large chest with a short-fingered hand. "What did you need from me?"

He fixed a look of confusion on his face and shuffled his feet with embarrassment. "I uh..."

She seemed to take pity on him. "You don't know where to go with that do you?"

He frowned. "I've been here one other time but these stupid boats all look the same..."

She laughed. "I hear you. Stepping to the back of the van she spotted one of her people returning from the boat with a bunch of empty containers. "You, Thomas..." She stuffed a pile of neatly folded linen tablecloths into the man's arms. "Take these to the dining room and show this man where the kitchen is."

Thomas slid Dolfe a weary glance and nodded.

He walked behind Thomas and averted his gaze as they passed the two dark-suited men standing at the bottom of the gangplank. As he'd hoped, the men assumed he was with *Delicious D'Lights* and didn't question his presence there.

If Dolfe had any residual doubts about his suspicion of Blanchette, after giving the two guards the once over, he no longer did. Their stance and manner were better suited to Secret Service than hotel security. The two men wore dark sunglasses that hid the fact their eyes slid continually around the area as if searching for hostiles, and though cleverly cut, their suits didn't quite obscure the guns they had strapped over their chests.

Dolfe doubted that Blanchette needed armed guards to keep a bunch of drunk twenty-somethings in line. It was apparent he had something else planned for the boat.

Entering on the aft of the *Lady*, they trotted down a short flight of steps that ended in a dark passageway.

"You're in there." Thomas pointed to a surprisingly large kitchen that roiled with white coats and frantic activity.

He inclined his head. "Thanks, man."

Thomas barely acknowledged him as he hurried down the hall with his linens.

Looking both directions, Dolfe ducked through a door and found himself in a large living area whose centerpiece was a circular couch covered in white leather. The furniture was positioned so that anyone sitting on it could look out the floor to ceiling window, which was shaped like the bow of the big yacht. Like the kitchen, the living space was busy. Five white-coated men and women worked to set up two bars with liquor, beer and wine. Another two people were putting bowls full of nuts and candy on the small, rimmed round tables, designed to keep things from sliding off onto the floor in rough seas.

Another woman, pretty, with dark eyes and hair and strong, Cuban features, was arranging flowers in several vases arrayed on a long, folding table. She looked up and smiled when she saw him. "Are you lost?" Her accent was strong, telling Dolfe she probably hadn't been in Miami for very long.

He smiled back, lifting the pan he held. "Kitchen?"

"Down the passageway, there."

He nodded, moving closer. "I was wondering..." He let his gaze slide over her appreciatively, his smile turning soft. "I've never been on a boat like this before. Do you think anybody would notice if I just had a quick look upstairs?"

Biting her bottom lip with uncertainty, she glanced toward the spiral staircase on the aft end of the enormous room. "I don't know..."

"I'll be fast, I promise. He reached into his pocket and pulled out his cell. "I want to get a selfie in one of the bedrooms." He waggled his eyebrows suggestively and she laughed.

"Here." She handed him a small vase filled with plump yellow roses. "These need to go on the table in the first bedroom. At least if you get caught, you can say you were helping me." Her dark eyes sparked with interest as he took the vase, letting his fingers slide over hers. "You're the best...ah."

"Rosalita," she supplied with a smile.

He felt guilty as she reacted to his flirting, but he told himself he was saving lives. A little harmless seduction was a small price to pay for that."

Dolfe didn't waste any time climbing the stairs with the pan clutched in one hand and the flowers in the other. He stopped at the top and looked down at Rosalita, catching her watching him with a speculative look. He pointed to the first door at the top of the steps.

She nodded.

Dolfe ducked inside, his gaze sliding quickly around the lushly appointed bedroom. White carpet covered the floor and a king sized bed, covered in black silk with white, red and black throw pillows was situated directly across from the door. Clear glass tables with curved bases stood at either side of the bed and a crystal chandelier sparkled above his head. If it weren't for the view of the yacht next door through the long, outside window, Dolfe wouldn't have even known he was on a boat.

He quickly set the flowers down on the long, black enamel dresser to the side of the door and opened the foil pan. He pulled out a loaded 9mm Glock and an extra magazine, stuffing the extra bullets in his pocket as he moved quickly around the room. The closets were empty, all of the drawers in the room and the adjoining bathroom were empty and he saw no signs that anyone had been kept captive there. He wasn't surprised, he hadn't really expected to find anything above decks. But he needed to search the whole boat. Just in case.

He started to leave and then remembered, stopping just long enough to get a picture of himself with the big bed in the background.

Then he cracked the door, peered down to the large room below, and found Rosalita across the room, her back to him. Dolfe slipped from the room and hurried down the hall to the next room.

Ten minutes later he exited the last room and stopped, blinking in surprise.

"What are you doing in there?"

11

*H*er heart pounding in her throat, Blaise pressed her ears against the door and clutched the thin, metal rod more tightly. Forcing herself to take long, slow breaths to calm her racing pulse, she wiped her sweaty palm on her pants and gripped the rod more tightly.

The voices started up again outside her door, a rumble of sound that played over her nerves like nails on a chalkboard. The guards had become increasingly jovial over the last hour as if anticipating something exciting...something fun...something that Blaise was pretty sure she was gonna hate.

A new voice, distinctive through the door only by the slight rise in octave said something that interrupted the rumbling laughter and the guards stilled. A moment later the lock was disengaged on the door to Blaise's prison. She glanced toward the closet across the room, assessing her handiwork with a critical eye.

It wasn't perfect.

But it would have to be good enough.

The knob turned and Bent's voice said, "Tell him to bring the car around. I'm getting her now."

Blaise closed her eyes and said a quick little prayer. *Please God, let this work.*

Bent stopped inside the door and she stilled, waiting to see if he'd take the bait.

"You were supposed to be ready."

Blaise gripped the rod more tightly.

"I'm talkin' to you, bitch."

In the silence Blaise's heart sounded like the gong of a bell. She prayed he didn't hear it.

Bent swore softly and came through the door, heading toward the dress which Blaise had stuffed with a pillow and positioned behind the closet door so it looked like she was kneeling on the floor. She'd even positioned the heels they'd given her to stick out behind the dress.

Bent had fallen for it. But she knew he'd realize as he approached that something wasn't right. She had to strike fast.

Blaise sucked in a breath and ran, the rod clutched in her hand and her gaze locked on the spot where it needed to go. She was six inches away, her arm swinging downward when Bent started to turn. He'd sensed her coming.

Or heard the pounding of her heart.

Either way the result was the same. He turned too soon, and the metal rod hit the lapel of his coat before glancing off and hitting flesh. The blow she'd practiced and planned so carefully wasn't nearly hard enough to cut through his throat. Not deep enough to do what she needed done anyway.

Bent made a guttural sound of pain and surprise as the metal sliced into his flesh, going only an inch before his hand came up and smacked her arm, sending the rod flying away from them.

Blaise barely felt the blow, she was flooded with adrenaline and fighting for her life. She launched herself at him, surprising him enough to take him down to the floor. Fists flying and knees straddling the much stronger man, Blaise managed to get in a few good strikes before he recovered.

Using the heel of her hand, she jammed it into his already bruised and swollen nose and followed that by jabbing him in the eyes with her fingers.

For a short, beautiful moment Blaise thought she had him. Blood ran from his nose and he couldn't open his eyes. But as she tried to push away...to shove to her feet so she could run...his hand snapped out and wrapped around her wrist, jerking her to a stop.

There was a shout beyond the door.

She was out of time!

Blaise screamed in pain as he twisted her wrist

and slammed her face into the floor alongside him. Tears slid down her cheeks as she writhed and fought against him, knowing she'd already lost. Bent jerked her arm up behind her and agony speared through her shoulder, robbing her of breath.

Blaise stilled, trying to breathe through the pain.

The only sound for a second was her soft whimpering and Bent's breath heaving in and out through his lungs. "I've about had it with you, bitch."

His weight shifted and Blaise saw movement as he lifted his arm, his hand curled into a fist.

She closed her eyes and waited for the blow, knowing it would hurt like heck and probably destroy her last chance to get away.

A second later there was a thud, like something heavy hitting flesh, and Bent's head slammed to the floor beside hers, his weight crushing her.

Blaise was afraid to look up. Worried that she'd find she'd just traded one predator for another. But a moment later Bent's heavy body rolled sideways and a small hand with manicured, ruby-red nails appeared in front of her. "Take my hand, Blaise. We need to get out of here."

The woman had wide brown eyes under a mop of curly, light brown hair. She was tiny, way too small to have taken down Bent. But as Blaise took her hand and allowed herself to be pulled to her feet, she saw the baton clutched in the woman's hand.

Standing beside her, Blaise's original estimation

of her height was too generous. If she was five feet tall Blaise would be surprised. "Who are you?"

The woman snapped her wrist, collapsing the baton, and grabbed Blaise's arm. "I'm a friend of Dolfe's. Come on. We need to go before somebody comes looking for this piece of trash." She kicked Bent's unconscious body and Blaise liked her a little better for it.

Though she was far too pretty for Blaise to like hearing she and Dolfe were friends.

"Why haven't I ever heard about you?"

They stopped at the door and her tiny rescuer peered through, searching the outer room quickly before jerking her head for Blaise to precede her. "We went to college together. I haven't seen him in ten years."

Blaise thought about this while she hurried after the other woman. "What's your name?"

"JJ. Now come on. We can chat later. Right now I need to get you out of here."

The outer door opened and JJ shoved Blaise sideways, through a door that led to a small, granite and slate kitchen. It was decorated like a man's kitchen. JJ leaned close, whispering. "I'm going to keep him busy and I want you to get out of here. Take the stairs, not the elevator. She shoved a set of keys into Blaise's hand. "There's a rusty white minivan parked in the outside lot. Take it to the marina and find Dolfe. He's searching *The Grand Lady*, looking for you."

Blaise didn't want to leave the other woman. She shook her head, opening her mouth to argue.

But JJ was already moving. "Do it, Blaise. Tell Dolfe where I am. Go!" JJ snapped her arm, extending the baton again, and disappeared inside the bedroom where Blaise had been captive.

Blaise stood there a moment, listening to the sounds of fighting through the door. She didn't know what to do. But in the end, she realized they would need Dolfe's help. And if Blaise was brutally honest with herself...all she wanted at that moment was to have her big, hunky Honeybun wrap himself around her and make it all right.

So she took off running. And prayed JJ would be okay until Blaise and Dolfe could get back to her.

Rosalita frowned up at him and repeated her question. "What are you doing up here? You're going to get me into trouble?"

Dolfe touched her arm and turned her toward the stairs. "Sorry. I just got carried away. Here..." He pulled out his cell phone and showed her the selfies he'd taken in each room, including one of him lounging in the massive tub in the main bedroom.

The photos finally teased a smile from her and she shook her head. "You've been busy."

Dolfe nodded as they hit the steps. "I'll be honest with you, Rosa..." He gave her his most winning smile, "Can I call you Rosa?"

Two deep, charming dimples appeared on her cheeks as she nodded.

"I wasn't telling you the whole truth before..."

Her gaze widened.

Dolfe lowered his head and spoke softly. "Catering isn't my only job. I ah..." A guy carrying speakers for the band setup walked by and inclined his head in greeting. Dolfe led her in the opposite direction. "I write a blog too."

Shock transformed her pretty face. "You're a reporter?" Her sexy voice lifted a few octaves, the accent deepening.

"No, no..." Dolfe shook his head, motioning for her to be quiet. "I'm a blogger. I have a blog called the Stealth Crasher. I kind of crash rich people's digs and then write about it." He grinned. "I have fifty thousand followers."

Shock turned to awe and Miss Rosalita lost a few degrees of iciness. "Really? *Mierda!*"

He nodded, walking her toward a door he'd spotted at the back of the large room. "So, if you'd do me a huge favor..."

She lifted a fine, dark brown eyebrow. "What favor?"

"I just want you to look the other way while I do a little snooping. That's all."

A shiny fingernail, polished a deep, dark brown, found its way between slightly crooked white teeth and she nibbled for a second as she considered his request. Finally, she sighed, muttering a few choice words in Spanish that Dolfe recognized.

They weren't words drawn from her happy place.

She surprised him by nodding. "Okay. But if you get caught don't tell anybody I helped you."

"Scouts honor."

Two tiny lines of confusion appeared between her brows but she shook it off, reaching to pick up a small vase of daisies from a nearby table. "Take this with you and if anybody asks what you're doing tell them you're looking for the Port side below decks head." She smiled prettily. "I don't know what a head is or my Port from my Starboard anyway."

Dolfe took the flowers. "Thanks, Rosy. A head's a bathroom. I'll put these where they belong, save you wandering around."

She nodded and turned away. Dolfe grabbed her hand.

"How do I get below decks?"

She hesitated only a second then pointed to the passageway. "Go toward the back of the boat. It's the door at the end of the passage."

"Thanks, beautiful."

He felt silly carrying the small, white vase of

flowers but they worked like a charm to keep anyone from questioning him. Dolfe found the door Rosy had described and ducked through it, jogging quickly down the stairs, which were hardwood with an oriental runner in forest green tacked to the center. At the bottom, dark hardwood floors were covered with matching rugs and the walls were painted a creamy white, the clam-shaped sconces on the wall giving off a soft light meant more for setting a mood than providing actual illumination.

There were several doors off the passageway. The one at the end was marked with a sign that said, *Engine Room*. Dolfe would save that room for last. It was doubtful Blanchette would try to keep captive girls there because the yacht's engineering crew would discover them.

The first cabin was a small head, elegant but spare. Dolfe left the vase and moved on. The second door was locked, but Dolfe had come prepared. Pulling out his lock pick set he had it open in a few seconds.

Dolfe searched the room quickly, finding nothing except the small amenities you'd expect in a decent hotel room. The second cabin was the same, as were the other two cabins on the starboard side. He was eyeing the engine room as he headed for the first door on the port side.

He quickly forgot it though as he reached to try the knob.

The door was fitted with an exterior deadbolt.

Bingo.

Dolfe's phone vibrated from the pocket of his jeans. He ignored it, quickly unlocking the door and slipping inside. The cabin was very different from the ones on the other side of the boat. There was no furniture in the room, except for a king sized bed that took up most of the space and one bedside table with nothing on it.

A single wall sconce, wide and rectangular, hung above the table and served as the room's only decorative light source. There were two small, oval portholes set high in the wall.

He quickly searched the two drawers in the nightstand and found boxes of condoms in the first one. But it was the contents of the second drawer that sent chills down Dolfe's spine.

Handcuffs, a small leather whip, scarves, leather masks, and other assorted pieces of leather that Dolfe didn't like the looks of. But the thing that worried him the most was the bottle of Rohypnol capsules.

Roofies.

Blaise didn't want to use garage parking so she parked illegally on Alton Street and jumped out, running toward Miami Beach Marina. There was a large white catering van parked along the curb. A woman in a white, caterer's coat was closing the back doors of the van as Blaise ran up. "I'm looking for *The Grand Lady*."

The woman glanced up, her round face moist and pink from the heat. "You're early for the party." The woman's gaze slid over Blaise's rumpled clothes to her sneakered feet. "You might want to come back in a few hours."

Blaise barely held onto her temper. She forced a smile. "Yeah, I will. I just want to know where I'm going tonight."

The woman's blue gaze narrowed but she finally nodded. "End of D Dock, in a side tie."

"Thanks." Blaise took off running, her heart pounding with fear. She scrutinized the marina looking for the men who'd taken her as she ran, knowing that the last place she should have been was that marina. But all she could think about was that Dolfe was there.

And she had to get to him.

She found D Dock and forced herself to slow down. It wouldn't do to draw attention to herself by running. *The Grand Lady* was a long, sleek white and navy blue craft with rope lines bordering the gangplank.

Two men stood at the bottom of the gangplank, eyes hidden behind dark sunglasses and stern faces staring straight at her as she approached.

One of them was the guy with the Flat Face from Blanchette's place. Blaise nearly turned around and started to run. Her heart pounded in her ears, her throat closing off with fear. What if he recognized her?

Dolfe could have already left the boat, which meant she was endangering herself unnecessarily. Blaise forced a smile onto her face and kept moving forward, even when Flat Face lifted his chin and started toward her.

"Hi!" She said in forced cheerfulness. "I'm looking for the party."

Flat Face cocked his head. "You are?" He smiled and Blaise relaxed. He was only flirting. He didn't recognize her.

The man leaned in and lowered his head, speaking softly. "I can show you a party, beautiful. Anytime."

Blaise's answering smile felt strained, stiff, but she placed a hand on his chest and laughed. "Sounds like I'm in the right place then."

He moved quickly, one hand wrapping around her arm with bruising strength. "Yeah, you are, Ms. Runa. You're in exactly the right place."

She gave a yelp of surprise and tried to wrench away.

A loud splash sounded nearby.

Blaise kicked out, her toes connecting with shin bone and pain jolted through her foot. He wrapped an arm around her waist and a hand over her mouth and pulled her into his body. "Let's get you on the boat before somebody sees us." He licked the side of her face. "I'd hate for somebody to misunderstand our playful little tussle out here."

Blaise screamed ineffectually behind his hand, kicking wildly. She tried jerking her head backward but he moved his head at the last minute, chuckling darkly. "Oh no you don't. I'm not Bent. I won't underestimate you, beautiful."

She bit his hand and he howled in pain, the sound cut off abruptly as something cracked against his skull. The man released her, sliding bonelessly to the ground and a big foot pressed against his hip, sending him over the edge of the dock. He landed over a tie-up and Blaze watched as the boat inhabiting the slip rolled into him, pressing him between its hull and the pier.

"He's gonna have bruises," a familiar, deep and sexy voice proclaimed.

Blaise's head snapped up and she squealed in delight, flinging herself into Dolfe's arms.

12

*B*laise covered his face with kisses, her body wriggling deliciously against him. Dolfe held her tight for one glorious minute, knowing they had to move but unwilling to give up the pleasure of finally having her in his arms.

Reluctantly, he pulled away, barely managing to keep a stern face as he admonished her for putting herself in danger again. "What are you doing here, Blaise?"

"Your friend sent me."

"My friend?"

"JJ. She rescued me from the hotel and told me to find you."

Dolfe swore softly. "Why don't women ever do what they're told?" Shoving his Glock into the waistband of his jeans again, Dolfe grabbed Blaise's hand and started pulling her along the dock.

She frowned. "Maybe because we're not dogs."

Okay, tactical error. Women didn't like being treated like they were weak. He stopped, turned, and jerked her back into his arms. He didn't care if Blanchette and his thugs showed up. He'd take them all on for just one delicious, reassuring taste of Blaise's lips. His mouth found hers and all of the turmoil that had been the last twenty-four hours tumbled away, lost under a tsunami of emotion that made the dock beneath his feet seem to roll and pitch.

Her taste sifted through him, sweet and powerful, and his lungs gratefully filled with her scent as he deepened the kiss, tilting his head so he could press her lush lips open, his tongue tangling with hers. Despite her hours of fear and stress, she still tasted like peaches and cream, her lush curves still felt like home.

It was Blaise who broke the kiss that time. She shoved him away, her gaze panicked. "I thought I was going to die."

Dolfe recognized what was happening. The adrenaline of the last hours was wearing off and, with safety in her grasp, it was all starting to hit her. He reached for her, wanting to calm and soothe. "I know, baby. I'm so sorry..."

Wringing her hands, she started to pace the dock. "He locked me up. He was going to..." One of her hands found her mouth and covered it, the fingers shaking as tears slipped from her sexy, brown gaze.

Dolfe knew exactly what they were going to do. The thought of his Blaise going through what Blanchette had planned made him want to kill and maim and then kill some more. He forced his hands to unclench and reached for her, grasping her hand and pulling her into his body again, wrapping himself tightly around her as she shivered and cried.

She was breaking his heart. Dolfe had known Blaise for nearly a year and in that time he'd seen her cry maybe one other time. His party girl was too happy-go-lucky for tears. But that free spirit...that devil may care attitude was gone...crushed under the touch of evil so vile Dolfe worried she'd never recover.

At that moment he'd give everything he had to have his party girl back.

"You're okay now, honey. I've got you. I won't let anything happen to you."

She shook her head, sniffling and dragging her hands over her cheeks to dry them. "It's not over. JJ's in trouble. She told me to run." Her wet, brown gaze lifted to his. "I didn't want to leave her there...she told me to get you."

Realization hit Dolfe in the gut with the force of a punch. JJ! He'd been so happy to see Blaise it hadn't registered what she'd said about JJ before. "JJ's been taken?"

Blaise sniffed again. "I don't know, but I think so. She only had a baton and that guy was a lot bigger than her."

Dolfe took a deep breath, nodding. He wrapped his hand around the back of Blaise's neck and pulled her close, kissing the top of her head. "Okay. Let's not assume the worst. JJ's smart and strong. She's been doing this for a long time. I'm sure she got out." He grabbed her hand and started off. "Come on."

"Where are we going?"

She stumbled along after him and Dolfe forced himself to slow. "To our rendezvous point. If she isn't there in a couple of hours I'll go to the Miami Beach police."

She stopped and pulled him to a halt with her. "Have you seen Dug?"

Dolfe frowned. "No. He called me this morning to tell me you were missing, but by the time I got here he was gone."

She looked so crestfallen Dolfe touched her cheek, wiping a tear from her soft, dark-chocolate skin. "I'll go see my contact at the MBPD and have him put a BOLO out on Richards. I'm sure they'll find him."

"Can we stop by the hotel first? I want to get my stuff and see if Dug came back."

Dolfe gave her a reassuring smile. "Sure. That's a great idea, honey."

Dolfe stood on the balcony of Blaise and Dugald's suite at the Crestview Empress Hotel, looking out at the ocean rushing against the shore. The room had been cleaned and the broken furniture removed, but there were still signs of Dugald's struggle that had made Blaise cry when they'd entered the room.

The sun was wrapping up the day in a burst of orange and pink on the horizon and Dolfe struggled to focus on its beauty so he wouldn't think about the gorgeous woman standing under a spray of hot water a single thin wall away. He slugged down the remaining finger of scotch and closed his eyes as it caressed his belly with warm fingers.

The whiskey should have soothed as it warmed, but it only made heat of another kind blossom deep in his belly.

He couldn't go there. Blaise had had a horrible day and the last thing she needed was an ex-boyfriend pushing himself at her. He might be able to talk her into it, but he wouldn't respect himself afterward.

"I'm out if you want to get in."

Shaking his head. "I'm okay. I'll shower in the morn..." He turned around and lost the rest of his response as all the air in his lungs fled.

Blaise stood just inside the sliding door, her long,

lushly formed body covered only in a towel, pebbled by silvery droplets. She smiled her secret smile and Dolfe's hard-won control fled him.

He glanced longingly at his empty glass. Just another couple of fingers of the golden fire might burn away the insistent craving gnawing its way through his belly. "It's not the right time, honey."

Blaise blinked in surprise, her pretty face clearly showing disappointment. "Oh..."

He suddenly realized how his response must have sounded. Setting the glass down on the railing, Dolfe moved closer, his gaze locked on hers. "Believe me, honey. I want to. Don't think I'm rejecting you. It's just..." He expelled a frustrated breath as his hand cupped her delicate jaw. Despite his best intentions, he found himself leaning close, his lips and body seeking hers in spite of what his brain told him he should do. "You've been through so much..."

Blaise fixed her sexy brown gaze on his mouth, her tongue sliding out to taste the fullness of her lush bottom lip. Dolfe groaned softly.

She touched his face, her fingers cool and soft. "Yeah. I was scared out of my mind. I thought I was gonna die, Dolfe. I thought I was gonna be..." Her teeth came out to worry the moist spot on her lip. "I was chased, manhandled, drugged..."

His pulse picked up, rage flared. "That bastard drugged you?"

She shook her head. "It doesn't matter. Nothing

happened that time won't heal. He didn't make me bleed. He just..." Her gaze flitted across the horizon, finding the ocean and its soothing push and pull in an obvious effort to stay calm. "He actually did me a favor."

Dolfe didn't realize she could still surprise him. He'd thought he understood her completely—loved her, cherished her—all the while recognizing that he couldn't live with her. He was wrong about so many things. He frowned, not sure he liked where their conversation was going. "Explain."

She stepped closer, her delightful form compressed against his.

His lungs deflated and his mind all but shut down. It was everything he could do to focus on her words. Because he knew, instinctively, that they were vital to him...to them...to their future together.

If they were going to have one.

"He said things that made me realize how stupid I've been...how selfish."

Dolfe's frown flew away on the wings of surprise. "Really?"

She chuckled, her breath bathing his face in sweet warmth. "It's not what he said. It's what he promised...what he represented."

Dolfe's hand slid over the satin curve of her back. "What did he promise, honey?"

A flash of anger sparked in her eyes. "Slavery, mistreatment, a very short future." She stared at the buttons on Dolfe's shirt for a long moment, her fingers twirling them thoughtfully.

His heart broke for her, even as he fought the need to tear the other man into tiny little pieces for the darkness he'd put into her sexy brown eyes. He stilled, waiting for her to go on. Because he realized at that moment that she needed to purge the darkness by sending it into the light. She needed him to hear it and how it affected her.

She trusted him to take the information and help her deal with it. It was more than they had shared together since the first night they'd met. A jewel wrested from the muck of her experience.

"I've always operated under the premise that I have lots of time. That my life was spread out before me like a huge buffet, filled with fun and emotional delights. Endless. I wanted to embrace it all. I wanted to taste—" She looked up finally, catching his gaze. Her eyes were filled with a question he read as *Would he understand*?

Dolfe told himself he'd do whatever it took to understand...because what they could have together would be worth it.

"I wanted to taste everything. I was so hungry... insatiable. Anything that got in the way of that I shoved aside. That's when I realized I pushed you away too, Dolfe. I didn't mean to...I... sectioned you off, relegating you to a corner, intending to savor you later. After I'd had my fill of the buffet."

As much as her words hurt...as much as he wanted to deny them...Dolfe didn't dare. He had some idea what it cost her to tell him that he hadn't been all that important to her.

Not nearly as important as her fun, her excitement.

He darn sure knew what it cost him. Finally, when it seemed she was waiting for him to respond, he nodded, stepping away. "I understand. I always knew we weren't well matched, honey. It's why I broke it off. But I realize now I really didn't mean it. I still wanted...want...you. I'm sorry I've made it so hard on you."

Tears sparkled in her eyes. "No." She touched her lips to his and sweet fire coiled through him at the touch. His hands flattened against the silky skin of her back and pulled her close before his brain realized the mistake.

Breaking that kiss was the hardest thing he'd ever done. He had to put physical distance between them before things moved out of his control. "Get dressed, Blaise. We need to get to the rendezvous point."

He thought she'd be hurt by his dismissal. He wasn't trying to upset her, but he needed her to step back, to let him let her go with dignity. He was walking the edge of a razor and a single wrong move would send him plunging.

He still needed to find JJ and Dugald.

After that he'd let himself crash. He'd lose himself in the pain and then try to find a way back.

It was an ugly choice, but it appeared to be the only one he had.

But she wasn't done with him. Blaise grabbed one of his hands in both of hers, tears spilling down her creamy brown cheek. "I never wanted to love you, Dolfe."

He suddenly couldn't take anymore. She'd come out there intending to give him a soft landing. He wasn't a soft landing kind of guy. She didn't want him. He needed to make the cut sharp and quick. "I get it, Blaise." He pulled his hand away. "You don't want me. Life's too short to be with someone you don't want." He started toward the door.

"Dolfe!"

He kept walking.

"Dolfe, damn you! Her hand wrapped around his forearm as he reached for the door. "I'm at the end, do you hear? I'm twisting on the last inch of a torn rope hanging over a pit of snakes."

He stopped, turning to blink at her. Amazingly, a smile tugged his lips. "Nice visual."

She bit the inside of her lip, probably to keep from smiling. "It works. That's exactly how I feel. I'm trying to tell you that I've been stupid to shove you aside. I'm trying to say that I love you...you big, stupid oaf!"

Hope soared but he didn't trust it. "Blaise, get dressed."

She punched him. Hard. Right on the nose.

Dolfe's head snapped back and pain blossomed across his cheeks and behind his eyes. "Ouch! Dammit, woman!"

She hugged herself and glowered back at him. "You don't deserve me, Dolfe Honeybun but I'm afraid you're stuck with me."

He blinked as realization hit. "You're serious."

She expelled a harsh breath. "Der."

Dolfe grinned. "You love me?"

Her glower softened. A little. "That's what I've been trying to say." She paced away from him, angrily stalking the large room. Blood ran from his nose but Dolfe barely noticed. "I'm pouring out my heart to you and you're all, 'we're not right for each other...get dressed, Blaise'."

Dolfe shook his head. "I thought you were breaking up with me."

She swore softly, "We're already broken up, you big lug." She slid her hands over the towel she was wearing. "Besides, would I come out here like *this* if I was breaking up?"

He shrugged. "I thought it was strange, but..." He touched his nose. "That really hurts."

Grabbing a tissue from the box on a nearby table, she stalked toward him. "Here. Don't be such a big baby, I...ahh!"

Dolfe grabbed her wrist and jerked her close, wrapping himself around her and capturing her sweet lips in a hungry kiss.

She grasped his broad shoulders, clinging to him as the world rolled out from under her, leaving her vulnerable and unsteady. But, then his lips claimed hers and she found her footing. *Him.*

Dolfe was her foundation in a roiling world. He was her balance. Everything else was just flash and color...pretty and enticing but ephemeral and ultimately unsatisfactory. Dolfe was real, he was substantial and his love was a gift so valuable, she wondered that she hadn't grabbed hold of it long ago and run.

She gave in to the pain she'd brought on herself...on both of them...and let the tears flow. Before she could stop it, a helpless sob escaped her lips.

Dolfe was undone by her tears. He always had been. She felt terrible for subjecting him to them, but he'd exposed an emotional nerve she couldn't seem to soothe. He'd given his heart to her months ago. She'd accepted the love and the beautiful benefits of having Dolfe by her side, but she'd withheld her heart from him. She'd spat upon his gift in an effort to hold onto something that ultimately had no value.

She didn't know if she could ever forgive herself for that.

But she did know one thing. She would make sure he knew how precious his gift was. And how very much she loved it.

"Hey, honey." Dolfe wrapped himself tightly around her as she sobbed. "Don't cry, Blaise. I'm right here."

She sobbed even harder at his statement and held on more tightly.

Dolfe's poor heart pounded hard and fast against hers. She was terrifying him. Blaise had to get a grip. Taking a deep breath, she scrubbed at her wet eyes and cheeks.

He smoothed a warm hand over her face. "What's wrong, honey. How can I help?"

She shook her head, sniffing. "You don't have to do anything, Dolfe. You're perfect. She leaned in and gave him a tender, lingering kiss. When she pulled away she offered him a smile. "I just realized what an ass I've been."

He frowned, apparently not liking her portrayal, and opened his mouth to argue. Blaise placed a finger against his lips. "No. Don't say anything. I need to talk for a minute."

He didn't look happy about it but he nodded.

"This whole thing has made me realize how

stupid I've been. All these months I've been chasing rainbows when I already had the pot of gold." She leaned her forehead against his. "I love you, Dolfe Honeybun. I think I've loved you from the very first time we met." She straightened, grinning. "When you pointed that big gun of yours at me and told me 'not to freakin' move'."

He waggled his eyebrows and chuckled softly.

She slipped her fingers through his golden hair, enjoying as she always did its silken heaviness against her fingers. "I'm going to spend the rest of my life if I'm lucky enough to have you that long, showing you just how much I love and appreciate you."

Dolfe's smile made the knot in her belly loosen and made her stomach tighten with interest. Unfortunately, they had other things they needed to do before she and Dolfe could begin building a new future together.

Dolfe seemed to agree. "I'm going to hold you to that, honey." He stepped away, leaving her body heavy with disappointment and unfulfilled need. "But right now we need to go save our friends."

She nodded, starting to turn away. "I'll go get dressed."

Dolfe grabbed her hand and yanked her back, wrapping his arms around her and kissing her with enough heat to make her toes curl. When he let her go, she stood blinking in a sensual daze. "Wow."

"Just giving you a starting point for when we get this other stuff behind us." He tapped her lips. "Hold that thought."

Blaise grinned. "I don't think I could let it go if I tried."

13

"Where are we going first?"

He pulled the dinged up minivan to the curb in front of the white monstrosity of the Miami Beach Police Department, parking it and glancing at Blaise. "*We're* not going anywhere. After I talk to JJ's cop friend, I'm dropping you at the rendezvous point and going after JJ and Dugald myself."

"Oh no, you're not. I'm coming with you."

Dolfe unfolded himself from the van and gave Blaise a stern look. "Stay here. I'll be right back."

He slammed the car door and started toward the station, grimacing as he heard the other door slam shut behind him. A second later her soft flip-flops slapped against the sidewalk as she caught up with him.

He didn't even look at her. "Do I need to define the word *Stay* again?"

"You can define it until you're blue in the face. I'm coming with you."

Dolfe reached for the front door and opened it, ushering her through. "You're very..." He caught her expression, lips compressed, eyebrow lifted, and changed direction smoothly. "—gorgeous in that tee-shirt and short shorts."

Her lush lips decompressed and curved slightly at the ends. "Thank you, Honeybun."

The uniform behind the Information desk looked up when they approached. "Can I help you?"

"I'm looking for Detective Lopez."

Blaise's head snapped up. "Jorge? How do you know him?"

Dolfe dropped an arm around her shoulders, kissing her ear. "He's a friend of JJ's."

Her eyes widened. "Dayum! I should have just let him help me."

Dolfe tugged her closer. "I wish you had, honey. It would have saved me about ten years off my life."

"Mr. Honeybun?" Jorge Lopez strode toward them, a paper cup of coffee in his hand. Shaking Dolfe's hand, his gaze slid to Blaise and he grinned. "Well, I'll be damned. You found her." He reached for Blaise's hand next, squeezing it. "Nice to see you again, Blaise."

"Thanks again for your help, Detective." If she

was embarrassed about dissing the cop before, she didn't show it.

Lopez inclined his head. "It was my pleasure." He turned to Dolfe. "I was just about to call you. I'm afraid we haven't had any luck finding Mr. Richards."

Dolfe's hand enclosed Blaise's and he gave it a comforting squeeze. "Have you searched Blanchette's apartment at the hotel and *The Grand Lady*?" he asked the cop.

Lopez frowned. "Not yet. There are politics involved. Blanchette has friends and relatives in very high places. I can't search without a warrant. I told you that."

Impatience made Dolfe's pulse spike. "How long before you get it?"

"I don't know. It's late. Judge Monak moves at his own pace at the best of times, after hours he's got snails passing him." Lopez glanced at Blaise. She was chewing nervously on a bright red fingernail. "We'll find your friend, Blaise. He hasn't been gone all that long."

"I'm afraid it's worse than that," Dolfe told the other man. He grasped Lopez's arm and pulled him away from the desk and the nosy uni there. "JJ's the one who found Blaise."

Lopez's dark eyebrows lifted in surprise. "Really?"

Dolfe nodded. "She was supposed to be doing surveillance and letting me know if she saw anything. But she went rogue on me and entered Blanchette's place alone."

"She probably saved my life," Blaise offered. "I'm worried about her, Jorge."

The cop looked worried too. "Tell me what happened."

Blaise explained in detail everything she remembered from the fight and JJ's rescue. When she was done, Dolfe and Jorge shared a look. JJ was in trouble. If Blanchette and his thugs were involved in what Dolfe thought they were, they wouldn't think twice about killing his friend. Or Dugald for that matter. "We need to get on that boat. There's a Christmas party tonight, whatever they're planning to do with Dugald and JJ, they'll do it tonight, while *The Grand Lady* is out on open water."

Jorge glanced at his watch. "I'll try Judge Monak again."

Dolfe nodded, turning away. "Drop by his house if you have to. This is life or death, Lopez."

"Where are you two going?"

Dolfe pulled the door open and placed a hand on Blaise's back, ushering her through it. "We're gonna go to a Christmas party."

Santa Claus wasn't feeling jolly at the moment. More like suspicious and worried. Dolfe pushed at his hair, which seemed determined to stray from the cheap white wig he wore and tugged on the too-tight sleeves of his rented red velvet coat. He was uncomfortable and felt way too conspicuous in the getup.

Santa's lovely elf was no help at all. She kept caressing his butt when she thought nobody was looking.

"Stop that, elf!"

Blaise's eyes sparkled beneath the blue-tinted contacts. "There was a piece of lint."

Santa lifted an eyebrow, fixing her with a stern look. "There seems to be an awful lot of lint on my ass tonight."

She wagged a long finger in his direction. "Now, now, Santa, no swearing." She leaned closer, twitching her nose when the shiny nylon strands of his beard tickled it. "Besides, everybody knows velvet picks up stuff."

"Yeah, I noticed the front of my pants just picked up your hand."

Blaise giggled.

Dolfe had to smile with her. It was good to see his sexy elf back in her element and enjoying herself. It helped that, in the hour and a half they'd been there they hadn't spotted Blanchette or any of his thugs.

Just a lot of horny women and drunk men with wandering hands.

Santa had nearly gotten in several fights already.

They'd had very little trouble getting past the guards at the gangplank. Dolfe had paid two drunk twenty-somethings fifty dollars each to flirt drunkenly with the guards as he and Blaise slipped past. When the guy at the door asked them why they were there, Dolfe had told him they were strippers— Santa and his Ho. They were gonna do a striptease later, after alcohol had warmed everybody up.

The guard grinned at that and smacked Dolfe on the shoulder, ushering them inside.

Easy peasy.

If only Lopez would call and tell him he had that warrant. They had the Coast Guard standing by just out of visual range, so they could move in if necessary.

He couldn't help thinking JJ was on the *Lady* somewhere, hurt and scared. The thought gave him the impetus he needed to move. He leaned close to Blaise and she tilted her pretty, sparkly face up for the kiss she expected. Even her lush lips sparkled and the pale pancake makeup she'd used had completed the disguise nicely. With the long, auburn wig and blue eyes, she looked like an entirely different...elf.

He couldn't resist lowering his lips to hers and, once he had, the kiss they shared lingered and heated, its sweetness turning Dolfe's cynical heart all gooey. He broke it and touched her chin. "Hold that thought, elf. I'm gonna try to get downstairs. If JJ and Dug are here that's where they'll be keeping them."

She nodded. "I'm coming with you."

"No. You stay here where you'll be safe. In fact, go stand in front of the band and don't move. Blanchette wouldn't dare drag you from such a public place."

She expelled a breath, nodding.

Dolfe started off and then turned, peaking a brow. "You're really gonna stay, right?"

She lifted her hand, middle finger extended. "Ho's honor."

Santa's beard quivered. "Did you just flip me off?"

Blaise looked at the rigid finger and shook her head. "This is the universal sign for Ho's honor. I'm shocked you don't know that."

He narrowed his eyes. "Mm-hm. Stay!"

"Woof!"

Ignoring her, Dolfe quickly headed for the passageway. A petite, Asian woman hurried up to him, champagne flute clutched in her tiny hand. "Santa, Santa, will you do a selfie with me?"

Dolfe bit back frustration and smiled. "Of course." He stood patiently while she wrapped herself around him and, holding the cell up said, "Say cheese!"

Her hand slipped over his buttocks and Dolfe gritted his teeth, reaching back to extract it. He held the offending hand up between them, to general hilarity from the woman's entourage.

She had the good grace to look embarrassed. "Sorry, Santa...I."

He dropped her hand. "Let me guess, lint?" When she giggled he nodded. "I get that a lot. Ho, ho and all that." Lifting a hand in a wave, Dolfe watched them pack together like a gaggle of giggling geese to see the picture she'd snapped and then, shaking his head, slipped into the passageway and headed for the door at the end.

"Yo, Santa!"

Dolfe jerked to a stop, an expletive dancing on his lips. He turned toward the voice and recognized the blocky form of the guard who'd questioned him and Blaise at the door. Forcing a smile, Dolfe lifted a hand. "Ho, ho, ho."

The second guy had too-long dark brown hair, a sallow complexion and pockmarks marring his cheeks. They moved through the passageway toward Dolfe. "Yeah, where is she?" the blocky, light-eyed guard asked.

The two men laughed as the first prickling of unease skittered down Dolfe's spine. "My lovely elf assistant is in the head. Is there a problem?"

The two men stopped in front of Dolfe. "Not at all. We have a small party on the upper deck that wants a private show." The man clapped a big hand on Dolfe's shoulder and tugged him toward the exterior door. "C'mon. We'll take a shortcut."

Dolfe pulled away. "I need to go get my elf."

The other guy slipped past Dolfe. "I'll go get the elf."

Dolfe yanked away again and started after the dark-haired man. "She's a little shy with strangers. I'll get her myself."

His muscles tensed, ready for confrontation, Dolfe spun as soon as the man's hand touched his shoulder, his kick catching the man in the gut and sending him to the floor gasping for air. Dolfe followed the first kick with one to the man's head and he folded to the floor, unconscious.

Dolfe pulled him into the galley and through, to the Chef's small office. He deposited him under the messy desk and checked him for weapons. Pulling a Sig from the man's shoulder holster, he stuffed it into his waistband where it was hidden by his coat.

When he came back out, closing the door quietly behind him, the entire galley staff was standing like pillars of salt, locked into mid-motion by the sight of Santa Claus dragging an unconscious man through the galley. He smiled. "Ho, ho, ho?" When that didn't make them feel any better, Dolfe explained, "Too much to drink. He didn't want the boss to know. He'll get fired for sure."

A couple of heads nodded. "Well, I'm off to entertain the masses." Dolfe headed back toward the party. He only hoped Blaise had held her position in front of the band.

Unfortunately, when he re-entered the room it was elf-free. Dolfe's stomach sank. He prayed she'd really gone to the head as he'd claimed. Unfortunately, it was more likely that she'd ignored his warning to stay and wandered off after him. If that was the case she was going to find trouble faster than Rudolf's nose could blink.

He checked his cell but the tracking software he'd quickly added at the last minute wasn't sounding the alarm. Dolfe wished he'd thought to bring the professional strength tracking devices he'd had at home. The cheap junk wasn't going to tell him where Blaise was until he was right on top of her.

He headed for the curving staircase to the upper deck. It was time to find out which private party was looking for entertainment. If it was Blanchette, he knew exactly how he'd entertain. The way he was feeling, a hearty round of Russian roulette might be just the thing.

"Keep it movin', darlin'." The pock-faced man had to shout to be heard over the sound of the boat's engine and Blaise realized the room would be heavily soundproofed.

Not good for her.

Blaise gave a yelp of pain when he shoved her, and her hip smacked into the edge of a metal pipe curving up from the floor.

The entire walkway was only about twenty inches wide, and the floor appeared to be made up of light-gray panels with metal handles. Blaise wondered what was stored beneath the panels.

As she was thrust toward the back of the noisy engine room, she figured she wasn't going to have a chance to find out. Praying the tiny, circular tracker Dolfe had given her to place in her bra was working, Blaise tried to stay calm and keep her eyes open, looking for any sign that JJ and Dug were there.

Ahead of them, a hatch opened and a man ascended a ladder into the engine room. Bent looked up as his feet hit the gray floor panels. Surrounded by black and purple bruises, his eyes glittered with malice. "Go time, bitch."

Pock-face pushed her again and she stumbled toward Bent. He shoved her to a stop before she hit him and she straightened, looking down into a room that could only be ten feet by ten feet at most.

A below decks hidey hole.

Bent grabbed her arm and propelled her toward the ladder. She barely caught herself before plunging headfirst into the room fifteen feet down.

"Tell Mr. Blanchette we've got her. We can finish cleaning up as soon as he gives us the go ahead."

Blaise started down the ladder, warning bells clanging in time to the pounding of her terrified heart, Blaise prayed Dolfe's little device could follow her through another layer of metal and soundproofing. Realizing it probably couldn't, Blaise did the only thing she could think to do. She reached into her bra and, turning to charge back up the ladder with a scream, dropped it onto the floor beside the hatch.

Just before Bent punched her in the jaw.

Pain blossomed as Blaise's head snapped back, and she felt herself falling back down the ladder.

14

*D*olfe was surprised to find the door to the first room unlocked. Two women looked up at him as he lunged through the door, surprise quickly turning to pleasure when they saw who it was.

The Asian woman patted the bed between them. "Finally. We were starting to worry that you weren't coming."

They both giggled at the woman's apparent double entendre.

The second woman, a statuesque brunette, crooked her finger in a come-hither sign. "I've been very naughty, Santa. I want to tell you all about it."

"Or show you," the Asian woman offered with a grin.

"Ho, ho, ladies," Santa said before ducking out.

The other rooms on the top level were empty. As

Dolfe was preparing to head below decks, his cell phone rang. He grabbed it out of his pocket, hoping it was Blaise.

It was Lopez. "Honeybun, I just got word the warrants came through. I'm going to pick them up now."

Dolfe opened the door a crack and peeked through. "Send in the Coast Guard, Lopez. I think they've got Blaise again."

The other man swore. "Have you found Joanna?"

"Not yet. I need to get below decks."

"No. Wait for the Coast Guard, Honeybun."

"Can't do that, Lopez. Tell them to hurry." Dolfe disconnected and slipped through the door. He had a plan. It wasn't a safe plan. It wasn't even a smart one. But it was the only option he had left. He was quickly running out of time.

Blaise shook off the muzziness in her head and looked around. To her surprise Bent hadn't come down the ladder to torture her. He'd closed the hatch and left her alone in the disgusting space.

She'd landed on a pallet, so the fall hadn't hurt her too badly, though her jaw ached and she was stiff and sore as she pushed to her feet. She climbed the ladder and shoved on the hatch, not surprised to find it locked.

Hurrying back down, Blaise forced herself to search the room for signs that JJ or Dugald had been there. She pulled the soiled and bloody sheets off the pallet and lifted it to look underneath. The room contained nothing else. The floor was covered in indoor-outdoor carpet, thin and stained. She wondered if there would be storage compartments under the rug if she lifted it.

The carpet came up hard and she found only fiberglass beneath it.

Blaise wanted to cry. If only she hadn't decided to do a little exploring of her own. She should have listened to Dolfe and stayed in the main room.

One of these days she was going to learn what the word *Stay* meant.

Until then she would make use of whatever she had left. She had her brains and her will to live...and she was really pissed.

She grabbed a dirty sheet and ripped off a long strip, a plan forming as she tested the strength of it between her hands.

It could have been only fifteen minutes or so before she heard footsteps and knew they were coming for her.

She quickly climbed the ladder and waited. As soon as the hatch was lifted, Blaise lunged. She registered the surprised expression on Bent's beat up face before she wrapped the torn sheeting around his throat and flung herself backward, down the ladder.

He hit the floor on either side of the hatch, his head slamming hard against the metal edging. Blaise let go of the sheeting and dropped to the floor, observing him.

Bent wasn't moving.

She climbed the ladder and shoved him out of the way, climbing into the engine room and pushing to her feet.

The cool muzzle of a gun found the side of her throat. "Smart *and* beautiful. It's too bad I can't keep you, Ms. Runa. You've been exceedingly entertaining."

She slid her gaze sideways to find Blanchette's handsome, smiling face behind the gun. "I'm surprised you're doing your own dirty work."

He looked surprised too. "You did see me take care of that little problem on the beach right?"

Blaise tried to focus all the hate she felt for him in her gaze. He didn't seem to care. "Where are my friends?"

Blanchette jerked his head toward the door. "They're waiting for us. Shall we go?"

She glanced at the floor and saw the little tracker. Hopefully, Dolfe would find it and know she'd been there.

Though she wasn't sure he'd get to her in time.

D olfe threw himself into the first door of the below decks rooms and it slammed open. A startled, middle-aged woman sat astride a naked, bald-headed man who was hand-cuffed to the headboard. The well-rounded female gave a startled shriek as the bald man wrenched his head up to look around her.

"Oh, sorry." Dolfe backed out the door, wishing he had eye bleach.

He tried the knob of the second door and found it locked so he opened it the same way. That room was empty but the bed showed signs of having been recently used.

As he headed for the third door he couldn't help thinking Blanchette was into a wide variety of kinky things. It wasn't too far of a stretch to see him kidnapping girls and offering them to wealthy busi-nessmen from around the world whose scruples were less...erm...scrupulous than they should have been.

He was preparing to put his shoulder into the third door when they finally found him. "This is very un-Santa-like behavior, Mr. Honeybun."

The pock-faced guard held what looked like a Sig Sauer fitted with a silencer toward him. "But it was very helpful of you to deliver yourself to us down here."

Dolfe thought so too. "Where is she?"

The man patted Dolfe down, taking the Sig he'd shoved in his waistband, and then jerked his head toward a door at the end of the hall, next to the engine room. "I'll show you. I'm sure she'll be pleased to see you."

Dolfe was pretty sure she would. But he had his doubts about the other guys. They probably weren't going to be happy. As he neared the engine room a rumble filled the air and the floor vibrated slightly. His gaze slid toward the door, realizing the noise would be good cover for anything unsavory that might go on there. He mentally berated himself for not searching the room more carefully earlier.

The scent of sea air, filled with salt and a tinge of ozone which promised a storm in the near future, rolled over him as Dolfe opened the door. A fine mist moistened his face as he stopped to get his bearings. He was standing on a large, teak covered swimming platform, complete with an aluminum ladder that arched above the deck and then trailed downward, into the black, agitated water.

Above his head, the band played on, the harsh, rhythmic base of seventies rock music throbbing through the night. Nobody in that room above would hear anything going on at the water line.

A bright yellow lifeboat was tied to the platform, bobbing angrily. His gaze swept the boat and, despite the dark, Dolfe immediately spotted her.

She was sitting in the front of the small boat, her hands and feet bound together. A silver-colored piece of tape covered her mouth but her gaze sparked with defiance. At that moment, Dolfe realized how strong she was, how resilient. And he was so proud of her.

Proud and terrified.

JJ sat behind Blaise, her head bowed. She looked pretty battered. She didn't even look up when Dolfe came through the door. Dugald was sprawled sideways in the back of the boat, one long arm trailing through the water. He wasn't bound because it was clear he was unconscious.

Blanchette stood on the opposite end of the platform, his stance wide, hands clasped behind him. He was smiling. Dolfe knew because he could see the flash of his teeth in the light spilling from the engine room door. "Welcome, Mr. Honeybun. Thank you for making it so easy for me to clean up loose ends."

Dolfe forced a smile, hoping it concealed the burning rage turning his muscles to iron. "Getting rid of the witness to your murder and all the people she talked to in one shot. Very efficient, Blanchette."

The hotel manager inclined his head in acceptance of the compliment. "Yes. I thought so."

Dolfe half turned as the Sig bumped his shoulder. "Put your wrists together behind your back." Pock-face held up a zip tie, and Dolfe realized he was running out of time. He'd have to make his move without the help of Lopez and the Coast Guard.

Sliding his hand into the pocket of the Santa Jacket, Dolfe let his muscles loosen. "I'm sorry to have to put a crimp in your plan." Dolfe pulled the small 38 Special he'd hidden in his belly padding and swung it, hitting Blanchette's man in the jaw and sending him stumbling backward.

Dolfe heard a splash as the man hit the water. He swung the gun toward Blanchette. "It's over Blanchette. The Coast Guard is on its way.

As if on cue, a wide beam of light swung across the water and painted the Port side bulkhead of *The Grand Lady*. A voice, enhanced by a bullhorn somewhere beyond the flash of light, was barely audible under the music. "This is the United States Coast Guard. Prepare to be boarded."

To his credit, Blanchette didn't look at all panicked. He calmly lifted his arm and pointed a gun at the lifeboat.

Dolfe stilled. "Come on, Blanchette, time's up. You won't get away with this."

Light flared over the water, missing the swim deck by about ten feet.

Blanchette's gaze drifted to the searching light and he smiled. "Oh, but I already have, Honeybun." He fired the gun and Dolfe's stomach jumped into his throat as Blaise screamed, the sound muffled by the tape over her mouth.

Rage swamped Dolfe and he fired toward the other man. Blanchette ducked sideways and then went down. Dolfe didn't wait to find out if he was still alive. The lifeboat was sinking more quickly than Dolfe thought possible.

Blanchette's gun went off again but Dolfe barely felt the sting of a bullet grazing his flesh as he dove toward Blaise.

15

*L*ight blazed over the swim deck and the megaphone blared again. "This is the United States Coast Guard. Drop your weapons and get down on the ground, hands and feet spread."

Dolfe was aware of the low growl of a small boat in the water, but he couldn't wait for them to arrive.

Blaise had turned to grab JJ as the boat started to sink. Fortunately, it was still tethered to the *Lady* so it didn't sink completely away.

With JJ hanging from her shirt, Blaise had captured the deflated rubber with her bound hands and was holding on as well as she could. Unfortunately, JJ was dragging at her, flailing around in an attempt to find something substantial. Blaise's gaze widened with fear as she started to tilt backward, into the water.

Dolfe flung himself to his belly and grabbed her before she went under, pulling her toward the deck.

Voices called out and footsteps pounded toward him across the deck. Dolfe looked up as Lopez joined him. "Help me pull them in. Richards was on the boat too, he wasn't bound but he was unconscious.

Lopez barked orders into his radio and divers jumped over the side of the rescue craft to begin the search for Dugald.

Between them, they got the two women into the boat and, seconds later, the divers broke the surface with Dugald between them.

"He's alive!" one of them yelled.

Dolfe pulled the tape from Blaise's mouth and kissed her. Her lips were like ice and she shivered uncontrollably. He figured it was more from shock than cold, but she gave him a smile. "What took you so long, Santa?"

Dolfe wrapped himself around her, warming her with his velvet-encased body. "My little bird fled her cage again. I've been looking all over for her."

He wanted to hold her all night, never letting go, but she was shivering so hard her teeth clacked together and Dolfe knew she was going into shock. She needed medical care. "Come on, honey. Let's get you off this boat."

Blaise nodded, allowing herself to be wrapped in blankets and handed into the Coast Guard's rescue craft. Richards was already in the boat and Lopez helped JJ in a moment later. He caught Dolfe's eye as he handed her down to a Coast Guard officer. "She's really out of it. They drugged her pretty good."

Dolfe looked across the deck, where two officers in dark blue uniforms had Blanchette cuffed and were questioning him. As if he felt Dolfe's gaze on him, Blanchette looked up. He smiled smugly and Dolfe's hands closed into fists. He took a step forward before Lopez stopped him with a hand on his arm. "Let it be, Honeybun. He'll get what's coming to him."

Dolfe frowned. He wished he was sure about that. But skunks like Blanchette had a way of weaseling out of trouble.

~

"He said what!?"

Blaise sat on Dolfe's couch and watched him, smiling despite the fact that his face was turning red and that big vein on the side of his neck was bulging.

Even enraged he was gorgeous and sexy.

"When?" He expelled a breath and nodded. "All right. We'll be there. Thanks, JJ." He hung up and stood staring out the window, a heavy snow drifting down beyond the glass.

"What is it?" she asked, twirling her reclaimed

diamond earrings as she watched him. Blaise caught herself chewing the inside of her lip worriedly, a habit that seemed to be leftover from the trauma of her recent experiences in Florida.

He finally looked at her and smiled, but his green gaze was intense. "Blanchette is making all kinds of accusations. He's claiming we set him up for the kidnappings and that he had nothing to do with them. They never found his gun. He must have dumped it into the water before they got to him. And he's hired the best lawyer on the East coast to represent him."

She frowned, her heart pounding in sudden fear. Events beyond their safe, little cocoon were threatening. Blaise had found her peace with the Blanchette thing since returning to Indianapolis. She and Dolfe had never been closer. She didn't want anything to destroy what they'd worked so hard to create. "Can he get away with that?"

Dolfe shook his head, his sexy green gaze haunted. "The problem is we have no proof. Without bodies..." Dolfe scrubbed a hand over his chin. "I don't think he can make his accusations stick, but he might be able to create enough doubt to walk."

Blaise shook her head, fear threading through her stomach, turning it to acid. "He can't walk, Dolfe." She chewed her lip harder, pain reminding her that she was doing much too much of that lately.

He came over and sat down on the couch,

limping slightly from the healing bullet wound, which fortunately had just grazed his calf. Blaise still nursed her own aches and pains from the world's worst vacation, but the most unpleasant of her injuries were emotional rather than physical.

Dolfe tucked himself in behind her and wrapped his arms around her as he kissed the top of her head. "He won't get off, honey. I promise. JJ and I are going to dedicate the next ten months up to his trial making sure of that."

"Dugald wants to help too." She chewed a fingernail just to give her poor lip a break, nibbling it as she thought about the trial. "We'll have to testify won't we?"

He rubbed a big, warm hand along her arm but didn't respond. He thought she wasn't ready to face that so he'd resisted talking about it. But Blaise was feeling stronger every day...getting her confidence back in increments. When the time came, she'd be ready. "I'm not going to let him get away with kidnapping, drugging and maybe even murdering all those girls."

Dolfe kissed her forehead. "I know, honey. None of us will."

They sat for a long moment, enjoying the sound of a blustery wind hitting the glass, the snow a beautiful, icy reminder that they were insulated and safe.

The multi-hued flash of tiny Christmas lights turned the falling snow into a light show, creating colored sparkles in the fingertip-sized flakes. Blaise smiled as she eyed the oversized evergreen tree she and Dolfe had manhandled into place in the tenth-floor apartment and decorated with ornaments from his childhood. They'd played Christmas songs while they decorated and Blaise strung popcorn for a cozy, finishing touch.

Blaise would nurture the memory for the rest of her life and she hoped they shared decades more Christmases just like it.

"We should get dressed. My family will be here soon."

Blaise lifted his hand and kissed the warm, rough palm. They'd decided to celebrate a delayed Christmas with Dolfe's family but, though she loved his family and the pleasant chaos they created when they all got together, she wasn't ready to share him yet. "Just one more minute. I want to pretend I can keep you all to myself for another...um...three minutes."

He chuckled. "Let's split the difference. I'll give you five minutes. In fact..." He slid out from behind her and reached for a package under the tree. "I was gonna give you this later but I just decided I want to do it now."

Blaise took the shirt-sized box and shook it, delight swirling through her. "I have no idea what this could be."

Dolfe grinned. "Open it."

Blaise ripped at the brightly colored paper, not even mentioning how horribly it was wrapped because she knew that meant he'd wrapped it himself and that made it extra special. Uncovering a plain white box that had been bent and torn in a clumsy effort to jam the two pieces together, Blaise pulled the mangled sections apart and grinned when she saw what lay inside. "You got me Santa undies!"

Dolfe shook his head and reached into the pocket of his shirt. "Those are actually Mrs. Santa undies." He slid off the couch and onto one knee, grimacing slightly as it pulled his wound.

Blaise's eyes stretched wide. He was holding the most beautiful platinum and diamond ring she had ever seen.

"Blaise Runa, would you do Santa the honor of marrying him and becoming Mrs. Claus?"

She stared at the ring, speechless with joy, and blinked as tears flooded her eyes. She was so surprised she couldn't move, couldn't breathe, couldn't think. She was locked in silent bliss.

Dolfe started to look worried. "Um, honey?"

She screamed, grabbing the gorgeous ring out of his hand and flinging herself into his arms. Dolfe managed to stay upright and his arms went around her as she sobbed happily on his shoulder.

"Yes! Oh my god yes, Dolfe! I've wanted to marry Santa since I was a little girl."

He laughed. "Okay, but did you want to marry Dolfe Honeybun?"

She shrieked again and, laughing, pulled away and put the ring on her finger. It was round, about three carats if Blaise was a good judge—and she was an excellent judge—and the slim band was covered in smaller diamonds. It was the most beautiful thing she had ever seen. Staring into his eyes, Blaise rubbed her hand over his bristly chin and sniffled as fresh tears slid down her cheeks. "I *do* want to marry Dolfe Honeybun. I think I've wanted that for a long time. I was just too stupid to realize it."

Dolfe stood and pulled her up with him. "For a minute there I thought you were gonna say no."

She stared at the ring on her finger and gave a happy little hop. "Not a chance, Honeybun. You're stuck with me."

He picked up the box with the red velvet bra and thong in it. The thong had a fringe of white fur around the top. "Aren't you going to try on your other present?"

She giggled, grabbing them up and heading for the bedroom. "I am. In fact, I'm going to wear them all night under my dress, so you'll know what's waiting for you when everybody leaves."

Dolfe hurried after her. "Maybe I should call and cancel."

"Not a chance, Honeybun. I want to tell everybody the news."

He grabbed her before she could dance away and she laughed happily.

Dolfe captured her lips in a lingering kiss. Blaise sighed as his addictive taste inspired her senses, turning her resistance to mush. When he broke the kiss she said, "I'm just gonna go try on my present to make sure it fits. Hold that thought."

"Future wife, I don't think I could let it go if I wanted to."

≈

Check out the entire Gainfully Employed series here: https://www.samcheever.com/series.html#gainfullyemployed

READ MORE GAINFULLY EMPLOYED BOOKS

Wait! You're not done! I have a gift for you. Please enjoy Chapter One of Book 2 in the *Gainfully Employed Mysteries*. **Murderous Craft.**

Dead End Job: When the only thing on tap is death.

A corpse discovered in a popular bar. An old acquaintance still nursing a mad-on from fifteen years earlier. And a cast of characters possessing secrets they'll do almost anything to keep. It's enough to make reformed (sort of) party girl Blaise Runa want to quit her dead end job. But in the meantime she fully intends to grab her sexy private eye fiancée and dig into the mess. Because she might be trying to *adult*, but that doesn't mean she's gotten any less nosy!

Murderous Craft

MURDEROUS CRAFT

If looks could kill, the woman across the bar would have already butchered Blaise and hacked her into a million tiny pieces. Something about her seemed familiar, but Blaise couldn't put a name to the face to save her life.

She narrowed her gaze at the woman and picked up another freshly washed wine glass, running a towel over the clear glass to dry it.

"Who you glarin' at brown sugar?"

Blaise held the hostile gaze across the room. "That chick's been glowering at me. I'm just trying to figure out who she is."

Tyrese Miller leaned an arm on Blaise's shoulder and followed her line of sight to the spot near the door. "I don't see anybody glarin' at you, Blaise."

Blaise slid the wine glass into the rack above her head. "That's because she just left."

Her boss lifted a dense, black eyebrow. "Mm-hm."

She turned a grin on him. "I'm not lyin'."

He chuckled darkly. "It was probably just some woman whose husband lusts after you, brown sugar. I wouldn't pay her no mind."

Blaise shrugged. "She seemed familiar but I can't come up with a name."

"Bronislava?"

Blaise frowned. "Huh?"

"That's a name. Here's another one. Shampooya." His trademark grin widened, showing a full mouth of straight white teeth except for a single gold one on the bottom. "Am I ringing a bell?"

She snorted. "I think your bell's already been rung. Those aren't names, Ty. Those are letters you shoved together to create nonsense."

He held up a hand. "God's truth. I saw 'em in a baby names book. They're real names."

"What in the world were you doing looking through a baby names book?" She lifted her brows. "Is there somethin' you need to tell me?"

Grabbing a frosty glass mug, Ty pulled a draft beer and settled it on the counter for the waitress swaying in his direction. "My brother's expecting. Well...his wife is...and they're having trouble picking a name."

"Hopefully they're not desperate enough to ask for your help."

"They have and I'm coming through for them. They now have a long, long list of intriguing names to select from. Personally, I'm leaning toward Exaltacion."

"Good Lord."

"Hey, it's biblical."

"So was The Plague of Locusts. Equally catastrophic."

The waitress reached the bar and grinned when she saw the beer sitting there. "Thanks, Ty." She was petite, curvy and sported a thick nest of dark brown hair which she was currently wearing loose and wavy around her shoulders. The waitress winked at the bar's owner. "How'd you know I was coming for that?"

He ran a cloth over a wet spot on the bar. "I've told ya a million times, Suz, I know all and see all."

Suzie Whotsnoggin turned a bright blue gaze on Blaise, widening it comically. "The man's delusional."

Laughing, Ty moved down the bar to help a customer.

Blaise grinned at her best friend. "How you doin' Suz?"

The waitress shrugged. "Okay. Tips are good tonight. But I'm dead tired. We didn't get out of here until three this morning. I swear, something's changed. We've never been this busy."

"I know, right? It must be this new line of local

beers. I think people like the idea of supporting the small breweries."

"Hey, gorgeous, where's my beer?" a masculine voice called across the bar.

Suz rolled her eyes. "Doodie calls." She picked up the frosted mug of beer. "You want to go shopping tomorrow? It's my first day off in over a week and I want to do something fun."

"I'll see what Dolfe's doing. If he's working I'd love to go. Mama needs a new pair of shoes."

"Doesn't Mama always?" Suz asked before swinging away. She swayed across the bar with the beer, large gold hoops in her ears dancing with her movement. Blaise watched, amused, as she deftly sidestepped her rude customer's groping hands.

Shaking her head, Blaise fought the coil of discomfort in her gut. She'd loved the atmosphere, lights, music and fun of working at Tyrese's Bar. But after six months some of the bloom was starting to wear off. To her ever-growing surprise, Blaise was starting to think she'd like to do something else. Something that would leave her nights free to spend with her honey, Dolfe. At least when he wasn't scoping out some cheating spouse or elusive thug.

Dolfe Honeybun was a private investigator who worked closely with the Indianapolis Metropolitan Police Department on the occasional case. He was darn good at his job and Blaise loved that he was that kind of guy. A big, strong man who carried a gun and an attitude and didn't take any crap from anybody. But between his hours and hers, they didn't get to spend nearly enough time together.

And since they'd only been affianced a few months. That was a serious problem.

"You're Blaise Runa aren't you?"

Blaise's head snapped up and her pulse spiked. She hadn't even heard the woman approach. "Oh my gosh! You startled me."

The woman didn't seem to care. She slid a hostile gaze over Blaise and frowned. "You don't remember me do you?"

"I'm really trying to." It probably wasn't a good sign that the most memorable thing about the woman was her frown. "Did I...annoy...you in some way?"

"You could say that. If sleeping with my boyfriend can be classified as an annoyance."

Kerplunk! The memory fell into place. Blaise leaned closer, narrowing her eyes at her accuser. The years since High School hadn't been kind...but Blaise could almost see the pretty face she once knew beneath the bags and wrinkles. "Dierdre?"

The woman put her hands on her well-padded hips and glowered up at Blaise. "You admit you slept with him?"

Blaise couldn't believe it was the same woman she'd been so terrified of. Voted most likely to irritate a rich husband. Head cheerleader. Came from a wealthy family who gave her everything she wanted. She seemed much smaller than she had back then.

Well...shorter anyway.

"I never slept with Roger White."

"Of course you did!"

Blaise shook her head, cocking a hip against the bar and crossing her arms over her middle. "Nope. We were just friends."

Dierdre Masterson slapped her hands on the bar top and leaned closer, wafting rancid breath that smelled like garlic into Blaise's face. "You must have slept with Roger!"

Conversations all around them stopped. All eyes turned to Dierdre and, by proximity, Blaise. Fortunately Blaise didn't embarrass easily. She chuckled. "I'm sorry to disappoint, Dierdre. I didn't."

"Then why did he break up with me!" she wailed.

The curious gazes slid quickly away, apparently unwilling to witness the train wreck at the bar. Blaise figured they'd hoped for salacious details but weren't comfortable watching Dierdre debase herself.

"I don't know the answer to that," Blaise said softly. "You'll have to ask him."

"I was going to ask him," the other woman said despondently. "But he stood me up."

Blaise stared at the lumpy woman sitting across the bar. She frowned, and then felt anger finally rise. "You asked him here to confront me?"

Dierdre Masterson shrugged. "I figured I'd be able to tell from the expression in his face when he looked at you."

"Good God, D, that was eleven years ago. You need to get over it."

The other woman's eyes filled with tears and Blaise instantly regretted yelling at her. "Would you like a drink? We have some really great local beers..."

Dierdre grimaced. "Not beer. I have enough of that at work."

Blaise's eyebrows shot upward. "You don't say?"

Seeing her expression, Dierdre laughed. She swiped tears off her round cheeks, sniffling. "I work at Byerson's Beers."

Understanding flared. "Ah. Those beers are some of our best sellers. Great stuff."

Dierdre didn't look like she cared. "Whatever." She sat in silence for a long moment and then glanced at Blaise. "What's wrong with me? Why can't I keep a man?"

Blaise panicked. The last thing she wanted to do was give counseling to a woman she didn't even really like. "Um..."

"Can I get you something to eat or drink?" Ty asked Dierdre. He winked at Blaise as he approached, nudging her to the side and putting himself between the pathetic woman on the other side of the bar and Blaise.

She could have kissed him.

"I don't want anything," Dierdre told him. Then she blinked and grabbed her purse. "Actually, you can do one thing for me. Have you seen this man today?"

She slid a photo across the bar to Ty. Blaise looked over his shoulder and was shocked to see a picture of Roger White in his quarterback's uniform.

"He's older now, of course. That was in High School."

Ty's lips twitched and Blaise surreptitiously pinched him below the bar. "Ow! Erm, no I don't think..." He picked the photo up, studying it more carefully. "Actually, I think I might have."

Blaise barely resisted blowing a disbelieving raspberry. He was clearly just humoring the woman.

Dierdre's scowl turned upside down and she looked almost pretty as she smiled. "Really? He was here?"

"Still should be," Ty said, jerking his head toward the restrooms. "I saw him head to the Men's a while ago."

"How long?" Blaise asked. "I've been here an hour and I haven't seen him."

Ty glanced at his watch and frowned. "You're right. It's been a while. I hope he's okay in there."

"Did he seem ill?"

Ty thought about it. "He seemed fine when I saw

him. He was even chatting up a pretty young woman a while ago."

Grimacing, Dierdre climbed down from her stool. "I'd better go check on him."

"You can't...um...ma'am..." When Dierdre ignored him, Ty widened his eyes at Blaise.

"I'll stop her." She rounded the bar just as the door across the room opened and a short, balding man with a veiny nose staggered out, looking like he'd seen a ghost. He lifted round, brown eyes to Ty and flapped a hand. "There's...oh God...I think that guy in there is dead."

ALSO BY SAM CHEEVER

If you enjoyed **Homicidal Holiday**, you might also enjoy these other fun mystery series by Sam. To find out more, visit the **BOOKS** page at www.samcheever.com:

Gainfully Employed Mysteries

Honeybun Heat Series

Silver Hills Cozy Mysteries

Country Cousin Mysteries

Yesterday's Paranormal Mysteries

Reluctant Familiar Paranormal Mysteries

ABOUT THE AUTHOR

USA Today and Wall Street Journal Bestselling Author Sam Cheever writes mystery and suspense, creating stories that draw you in and keep you eagerly turning pages. Known for writing great characters, snappy dialogue, and unique and exhilarating stories, Sam is the award-winning author of 80+ books.

To learn more about Sam and her work, visit her at one of her online hotspots:
www.samcheever.com
samcheever@samcheever.com